"I am so sure that I can make you gasp with desire, so sure I can make you explode with pleasure, that if I am wrong, Laney, I will pay you ten million dollars."

Ten million dollars.

The amount staggered her. She thought of what it would mean. She could go back to New Orleans and hire full-time caregivers for her father. Her grandmother, who'd worked her fingers to the bone for fifty years, could finally relax and enjoy her life. Laney could be with the family she loved.

"But the amount I'll pay if I lose doesn't matter." Kassius looked down at her, his eyes glinting wickedly in the moonlight. "Because I intend to win."

Laney licked her lips. "Just for the sake of argument, if you do make me, um... If you prove I'm not frigid, then what would you want in return?"

"Beyond the sweet prize of your body?" He moved suddenly, leaning over the bed, running his wide hand in a sensual stroke down her body. His expression was deadly serious. "If I cannot give you pleasure, Laney, I will give you ten million dollars, and you will walk out of here a wealthy woman. But if I make you explode with joy, you will surrender everything. You will allow me to take possession of your body and fill you with my child. You will be mine—forever."

Wedlocked!

Conveniently wedded, passionately bedded!

Whether there's a debt to be paid, a will
to be obeyed or a business to be saved...
she's got no choice but to say "I do!"

But these billionaire grooms have got another
think coming if they imagine the marriage
will be that easy...

Soon their convenient brides become
the object of an *inconvenient* desire!

Find out what happens after the vows in

The Billionaire's Defiant Acquisition
by Sharon Kendrick

One Night to Wedding Vows
by Kim Lawrence

Expecting a Royal Scandal
by Caitlin Crews

Trapped by Vialli's Vows
by Chantelle Shaw

Look out for more **Wedlocked!** stories
coming soon!

Jennie Lucas

BABY OF HIS REVENGE

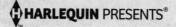

Recycling programs
for this product may
not exist in your area.

ISBN-13: 978-0-373-13473-1

Baby of His Revenge

First North American Publication 2016

Copyright © 2016 by Jennie Lucas

Printed in U.S.A.

USA TODAY bestselling author **Jennie Lucas**'s parents owned a bookstore and she grew up surrounded by books, dreaming about faraway lands. A fourth-generation Westerner, she went east at sixteen to boarding school on scholarship, wandered the world, got married, then finally worked her way through college before happily returning to her hometown. A 2010 RITA® Award finalist and 2005 Golden Heart® Award winner, she lives in Idaho with her husband and children.

Books by Jennie Lucas

Harlequin Presents

A Ring for Vincenzo's Heir
Nine Months to Redeem Him
Uncovering Her Nine Month Secret
The Sheikh's Last Seduction
To Love, Honor and Betray
A Night of Living Dangerously
The Virgin's Choice
Bought: The Greek's Baby

At His Service

The Consequences of That Night

Princes Untamed

Dealing Her Final Card
A Reputation for Revenge

One Night In...

Reckless Night in Rio

Unexpected Babies

Sensible Housekeeper, Scandalously Pregnant

Visit the Author Profile page at Harlequin.com for more titles.

To Pete, who inspires me every day.

CHAPTER ONE

"I SHOULD FIRE you right now, Laney." Her boss glared at her. "Anyone would love to have your job. All of them less stupid than you!"

"I'm sorry!" Laney May Henry had tears in her eyes as she saw the hot coffee she'd just spilled on her boss's prized white fur coat, which had been hanging on the back of a chair. Leaning forward, she desperately tried to clean the stain with the hem of her faded cotton shirt. "It wasn't..."

"Wasn't what?" Her boss, a coldly beautiful American-born countess who had been married and divorced four times, narrowed her carefully made-up eyes. "What are you trying to imply?"

It wasn't my fault. But Laney took a deep breath. She knew there was no point in telling her boss that her friend had deliberately tripped her as she'd brought them coffee. No point, because her boss had seen the whole thing and had laughed along with her friend as Laney tripped with a noisy *oof,* sprawling helter-skelter across the carpet of the lavish Monaco flat. For her boss, it had all been a good joke—until she saw the coffee hit her full-length fur coat.

"Well?" Mimi du Plessis, the Comtesse de Fourcil, demanded. "I'm waiting."

Laney dropped her gaze. "I'm sorry, Madame la Comtesse."

Her boss turned to her friend, dressed in head-to-toe Dolce and Gabbana on the other side of the white leather sofa, smoking. "She's stupid, isn't she?"

"Very stupid," the friend agreed, daintily puffing out a smoke ring.

"So hard to get good help these days."

Biting her lip hard, Laney stared down at the white rug. Two years ago, she'd been hired to organize Mimi du Plessis's wardrobe, keep track of her social engagements and run errands. But Laney had quickly discovered why the salary was so good. She was on call day and night, often needing to work twenty-hour days and endure her boss's continual taunts. Every day of the last two years, Laney had fantasized about quitting and going back to New Orleans. But she couldn't. Her family desperately needed the money, and she loved her family.

"Take the fur and get out of here. I can't stand to look at your pathetic little face another moment. Get the coat to the cleaners and heaven help you if it's not back before the New Year's Eve gala tonight." Dismissing her, the comtesse turned back to her friend, resuming their earlier conversation. "I think tonight Kassius Black will finally make his move."

"You think so?" her friend said eagerly.

The comtesse smiled, like a smug Persian cat with a golden bowl of overpriced cream. "He's already wasted millions of euros giving anonymous loans to my boss. But the way things are going, my boss's company will be bankrupt within the year. I finally told Kassius that if he wants my attention, he should stop throwing money down the drain and just ask me out."

"What did he say?"

"He didn't deny it."

"So he's taking you to the ball tonight?"

"Not exactly…" She shrugged. "But I was tired of waiting for him to make his move. It's obvious he must be wildly in love with me. And I'm ready to get married again."

"Married?"

"Why not?"

Her friend pursed her lips. "Darling, yes, Kassius Black is rich as sin and dangerously handsome, but who *is* he? Where does he come from? Who are his people? No one knows."

"Who cares?" Mimi du Plessis, who liked to brag about how she could trace her family history back not only to the Mayflower, but to Charlemagne, now shrugged it off. "I'm fed up with aristocrats without a single dollar to their name. My last husband, the comte, bled me dry. Sure, I got his title—but after the divorce I had to get a job. Me! *A job!*" She shuddered at the indignity, then brightened. "But once I'm Kassius Black's wife, I'll never have to worry about working again. He's the tenth-richest man in the world!"

Her friend elegantly blew out another smoke ring. "Ninth. His real estate investments have exploded."

"Even better. I know he'll try to kiss me at midnight. I can't wait. You can just tell any wife of his would be well satisfied in bed…" Her sharp face narrowed when she saw Laney still hesitating unhappily by the sofa, heavy coat in her arms. "Well? What are you still doing here?"

"I'm sorry, madame, but I need your credit card."

"Give you my card? That's a joke. Pay for it yourself. And get us more coffee. Hurry up, you idiot!"

Beneath the weight of the white fur coat, Laney took the elevator downstairs and trudged through the lobby of the elegant Hôtel de Carillon onto the most expensive street in Monaco, filled with designer shops, overlooking the famous Casino de Monte Carlo and the Mediterranean Sea. As she walked out of the exclusive residential hotel, the doorman gave her an encouraging smile. "Ça va, Laney?"

"Ça va, Jacques," she replied, mustering up a smile. But the heavy gray clouds seemed as leaden as her heart.

It had just stopped raining. The street was wet and so were the expensive sports cars revving by, along with the sodden-looking tourists crowded together in packs on the sidewalk. In late December, the winter afternoons were short and the nights were long. But that only added to the delight of New Year's Eve. It was a popular time for people, especially wealthy yacht owners, to visit Monaco and enjoy exclusive parties, designer shops and world-class restaurants.

Laney comforted herself with the thought that at least the rain had stopped. Aside from her worries about the coat getting wet, she'd run out of the building too fast to grab her coat and just wore a plain white shirt, loose khakis and sensible clogs with her dark hair pulled up in a ponytail—the uniform of the servant class. But even without rain, the air was damp and chilly, and the sun was weak. Shivering, she held the fur coat tightly in her arms, both to protect it from being splashed by a passing car and to keep herself warm.

She didn't like her boss's fur coats much. They reminded her too much of the pets she'd loved growing up at her grandmother's house outside New Orleans, the sweet, dopey old hound dogs and proudly independent cats. They'd comforted her through some heartbreaking days as a teenager. Thinking of them reminded Laney of everything else she missed about home. A lump rose in her throat. It had been two years since she'd last seen her family.

Don't think about it. She took a deep breath. The fur in her arms was bulky and big, and Laney was on the petite side, so she shifted the coat over her shoulder to look down at her smartphone.

But as she scouted out the nearest fur cleaner, she was suddenly jostled by a large group of tourists stampeding by, blindly following their guide's flag up ahead. Stumbling forward, Laney tripped off the curb and fell forward into the street. Turning with a gasp, as if in slow motion, she saw a red sports car barreling down on her!

There was a loud squeal of tires, and Laney felt a surge of regret that she was going to die, at twenty-five, far from home and everyone she loved, holding her boss's dirty fur coat, run over by a car. She just wished she could tell her grandmother and her father one last time that she loved them…

She closed her eyes and held her breath as she felt the impact. The car knocked her over the hood and she flew, then fell hard on something soft.

The air was knocked out of her lungs, and she wheezed for breath as everything went dark.

"Damn you, what were you thinking!"

It was a man's voice. It didn't sound like the voice of God, either, so she couldn't be dead. Laney's eyes fluttered open.

A man was standing over her, looking down. His face and body were hidden in shadow, but he was tall, broad-shouldered. And, it seemed, angry.

A crowd gathered around them as the man knelt beside her.

"Why did you run out in the street like that?" The man was dark-haired, dark-eyed, handsome. "I could have killed you!"

Laney suddenly recognized him. Coughing, she sat up abruptly. A wave of dizziness went through her, and she put her hand on her head, feeling sick.

"Be careful, damn you!"

"Kassius—Black," she croaked.

"Do I know you?" he said tersely.

Why would he? She was nobody. "No…"

"Are you injured?"

"No," she whispered, then realized to her shock that it was true. Looking down, she saw the fur had blocked her impact against the street like a soft pillow. Incredulously, she touched the nose of the wildly sleek and expensive sports car pressing into her shoulder. He must have stopped on a dime.

"You're in shock." Without asking permission, he ran his hands over her. He was no doubt searching for broken bones, but having him touch her—stroking her arms, her legs, her shoulders—caused heat to flood through Laney. Her cheeks burned, and she pushed him away.

"I'm fine."

He looked at her skeptically.

She look a shuddering breath and tried to smile. "Really."

Of all the billionaires in Monaco—and there were tons—she'd just inconvenienced the one her boss wanted, this mysterious and dangerous man. If the comtesse found out Laney had caused *him* problems, on top of everything else...

Laney tried to stand up.

"Wait," he barked. "Take a breath. This is serious."

"Why?" She glanced back at the glossy fender of the car. "Did I hurt your Lamborghini?"

"Funny." His voice was dry. He was looking at her narrowly. "What were you thinking, jumping in front of me?"

"I tripped."

"You should have been more careful."

"Thanks." Rubbing her elbow, she winced. On the two occasions she'd seen the man before, while he was having lunch meetings with the comtesse, Laney had vaguely thought Kassius Black must be an American raised in Europe, or possibly a European raised in America. But there was a strange inflection in his voice that didn't suit either theory. In fact, it was an accent she recognized well. But it obviously wasn't possible. She rubbed her forehead. She must have hit it harder than she thought. "I'll try to take your advice in the future."

Rising to his feet, he looked around at the crowd that had formed a semicircle around them in the street. "Is there a doctor?" No one moved, even when he repeated the request in rapid succession in three other languages. He pulled his phone from his pocket. "I'm calling an ambulance."

"Um..." She bit her lip. "That's nice and all, but I'm afraid I don't have time for that."

He looked incredulous. "You *don't have time* for an ambulance?"

She gave herself a quick look for gushing blood or maybe a broken leg she hadn't noticed. But the worst that seemed to have happened was that she'd had the wind knocked out of her and had gotten a little lump on her forehead. She touched it. "I'm on an urgent errand for my boss."

Wincing a little, she pushed herself off the street and rose to her feet. He reached out his hand to help her. When their hands touched, she felt electricity course through her body, making her shake all over. She looked up at him. He was nearly an entire foot taller than she was, handsome and powerful and sleek in his dark suit. She could only imagine what a pathetic mess she looked like right now. Talk about *noblesse oblige*.

She dropped his hand.

"Well, thanks for stopping your car," she muttered. "I'd better get going..."

"Who's your boss?"

"Mimi du Plessis, the Comtesse de Fourcil."

"Mimi?" Abruptly, the man stepped closer, searching her face. Recognition dawned. "Wait. I know you now. The little mouse who scampers around Mimi's flat, fetching her slippers and finding her phone."

Laney blushed. "I'm her assistant."

"What was her errand, so important that you nearly died for it?"

"But I didn't die."

"Lucky for you."

"Lucky," she breathed as she tilted her head back. Her mind felt oddly blank as she looked up at him. Up close, he was even more handsome. And his face had character, with an interesting scar across one of his high cheekbones. His aquiline nose was slightly uneven at the top, as if it had been broken when he was young and not properly realigned. This man hadn't been born rich—that much was for sure. He was nothing like the wealthy playboys Mimi had gone through like tissue paper since her divorce. This man was a fighter. A thug, even. And for some reason, as he looked down at her, he made Laney feel dizzy—as if the world had just moved beneath her sensible shoes.

His gaze sharpened. "So what was the errand, little mouse," he repeated, "so important you were willing to die for it?"

"Her coat—" That reminded her. Looking around for it, she gave an anguished cry.

The expensive white fur was now soaked in a muddy puddle on the street, ripped to shreds where one of his tires had gone through it.

Laney took a deep breath.

"I'm so fired," she whispered. Her head was starting to clang with headache as she knelt and picked it up. "She told me to get it cleaned before the ball tonight. Now it's ruined."

"It's not your fault."

"But it is," she said miserably. "First I spilled coffee on it. Then I wasn't paying attention where I was walking. I was too busy looking at my phone to get directions to a cleaner... My phone!"

Looking around wildly, she saw it had been crushed beneath the back wheel of his car. Going to it, she lifted its crumpled form into her hands. Tears rose in her eyes as she looked at its shattered face, now crushed into unrecognizable metal.

She wouldn't let herself cry. She couldn't.

Then just when she thought things couldn't get worse, the gray clouds burst above them, and it started to rain.

It was too much. She felt cold raindrops pummeling her messed-up hair and chilled, bruised body. It was the final straw. Against her will, she started to laugh.

Kassius Black looked at her like she was crazy. "What's so funny?"

"I'll definitely lose my job for this," she gasped, hardly able to breathe for laughing.

"And you're happy about it?"

"No," she said, wiping her eyes. "Without my job, my family won't be able to pay rent next month or my dad pay for his medications. It's not funny at all."

Kassius's eyes turned cool. "I'm sorry."

"Me, too," she replied, thinking what a strange conversation this was to have with the ninth-richest man in the world. Or was it the tenth?

A car honked, and she jumped. They both turned to look. The crowds of people around them had already started to disperse now it was clear she wasn't going to bleed out and die on the street. But his car was still holding up traffic. The drivers of the similarly expensive cars lined up behind it were starting to get annoyed.

Kassius's jaw clenched as he made a rude gesture to them then turned back to her. "If you're not hurt and don't want to see a doctor—" he watched her carefully "—then I guess I will be on my way."

"'Bye," Laney said, still mourning her broken phone. "Thanks for not killing me."

Turning away from him, she dropped the fragments of metal in a corner trash can. Slinging the ruined fur over her shoulder, Laney started to walk desolately down the sidewalk in the pouring rain. She'd go back to the Hôtel de Carillon and ask Jacques if he knew a fur cleaner that could perform magic. Oh, who was she kidding? Magic? He'd need to turn back time.

She felt someone grab her arm. Looking up in surprise, she saw Kassius, his handsome face grim. He said through gritted teeth, "All right, how much do you want?"

"How much of what?"

"Just get in my car."

"I don't need a ride—I'm just going back to the Hôtel de Carillon."

"To do what?"

"Give my boss her fur back and let her yell at me and then fire me."

"Sounds like fun." Lifting a dark eyebrow, he ground out, "Look. It's obvious you threw yourself in front of my car for a reason. I don't know why you're not doing the obvious thing and immediately asking for money, but whatever your game is—"

"There's no game!"

"I can solve your problem. About the coat."

Laney sucked in her breath. "You know how to get it fixed? In time for the ball tonight?"

"Yes."

"I would be so grateful!"

His voice was curt. "Get in."

By this time, the cars behind them weren't just honking, but the drivers were yelling impolite suggestions.

Kassius held open the passenger door, and she climbed in, still clinging to the ruined, muddy, ripped fur coat. He climbed into the driver's seat beside her, and without bothering to respond to the furious drivers behind them, he drove off with a low roar of his sleek car's powerful engine.

She glanced at him as they drove. "Where are we going?"

"It's not far."

"My grandma would yell at me if she knew I'd gotten in a car with a stranger," she said lightly. But part of her was already wondering if she should have refused his offer. The fact that he drove an expensive car didn't mean he could be trusted—in fact, in her admittedly limited experience, it generally meant the opposite.

"We're not strangers. You know my name."

"Mr. Black—"

"Call me Kassius." He gave her a dark sideways glance. "Though I don't think Mimi ever introduced us."

"All right. Kassius." The name moved deliciously on her tongue. She licked her lips. "I'm Laney. Laney May Henry."

"American?"

"From New Orleans."

His sudden look was so sharp and searching that it bewildered her. She wasn't accustomed to being noticed by men, and especially not a man like him. She felt Kassius Black's attention all the way to her toes.

Her boss had said the man was inscrutable, that he had ice water in his veins. Why was he bothering to help her?

But she needed his help too badly to ask questions right now. "Thank you for helping me. You're being very kind."

"I'm not kind," he said in a low voice. He looked at her. "But don't worry. You won't lose your job."

Her heart lifted to her throat. She couldn't remember the last time anyone had helped her. Generally she was the one who was responsible for everyone and everything.

"Thank you," she repeated, her voice cracking slightly as she looked out the window, blinking rapidly.

Monaco was a small principality, only two square kilometers, pressed against the Mediterranean Sea on one side, surrounded by France on the other. But as the country had no income tax, wealthy people from all over the world had flocked to become citizens, so it was said that a third of the population were now millionaires. It was famous for its nineteenth-century grand casino, its elegant society and the Grand Prix held every year on the notoriously winding streets.

"I don't see how this can possibly be made perfect again," she said sadly, looking at the ragtag coat in her arms. She looked at him. "Maybe you could come back with me to her suite and explain what happened? If you put in a good word, then the comtesse wouldn't fire me."

His voice was cool as he focused on the road. "Mimi and I are business acquaintances, nothing more. What makes you so sure I'd have influence on her?"

"Aren't you in love with her?" Laney blurted out.

"In love!" His hands clenched on the steering wheel, causing the car to sway slightly on the road. Then he looked at her. "What gave you that idea?"

Laney realized she'd gotten it by eavesdropping, and her cheeks went hot. She didn't want to be indiscreet or spread rumors about her boss. Embarrassed, she shrugged, looking out at the pouring rain. "Most men seem to fall in love with her. I just assumed…"

"You assumed wrong." He pulled the car abruptly into a spot on the street and parked. "In fact, I've been accused of having no heart."

"That's not true." She smiled at him shyly. "You must have one. Why else would you be helping me?"

He gave her a darkly inscrutable glance. Without answer, he turned off the engine and got out of the car.

Laney's heart pounded as he swiftly strode around the front of the car. He was very tall, at least a foot taller than her, and probably a hundred pounds heavier—a hundred pounds of pure lean muscle. But in spite of his muscle, he moved with almost feline grace beneath his sleek dark suit. Opening her door, he held out his hand.

She stared at it in consternation, wondering if she dared to put her hand in his when it had caused such a powerful reaction in her before.

"Fur?" He said impatiently.

Oh. Blushing, she handed it out to him. He threw the coat casually over his shoulder. It seemed small compared to him. He reached out his hand again. "You."

For a moment Laney hesitated. She was afraid to make a fool of herself, and the chance seemed high. When she was nervous, she always blurted out stupid things, and Kassius Black made her very nervous.

She timidly placed her hand in his and let him help her out. The warmth and strength of his larger hand against hers did all kinds of strange things to her insides. Dropping his hand quickly, she looked up at the Beaux Arts–style building with a frown. "This doesn't look like a dry cleaner's."

"It's not. Follow me."

She followed him through the doors of a very elegant designer boutique. He handed the old fur to the first salesgirl he saw standing inside. "Here. Get rid of this."

"Of course, sir," she replied serenely.

"*Get rid of it?* What are you doing?" Laney cried. "We can't throw it away!"

But he was looking at the beautiful, well-dressed salesgirl. "Get us a new coat just like it."

"What?" said Laney.

"Of course, sir," the girl repeated calmly, and Laney had the sense that her courteous response would have been the same to the request of any wealthy customer, whether it involved tossing a candy wrapper or disposing of a dead body. "We do have one very similar from the same line. The cost is fifty thousand euros."

Laney nearly staggered to her knees, but Kassius didn't blink.

"We'll take it to go."

Ten minutes later, he was driving her back to the Hôtel de Carillon with the elegantly wrapped new ermine tucked in the trunk, which was confusingly in the front of the car, not the back. Rich people always did some things a little differently, she thought.

But there were some things they did the same.

"There's only one reason you'd blow all that money on a coat," Laney informed him as he drove. "Admit it. You're wildly in love with the comtesse."

Kassius glanced at her out of the corner of his eye. "I didn't do it for her." He gave her a sudden grin. "I did it for you."

"Me?"

"You know who I am and the resources I have. And yet you haven't tried to take advantage of the fact that I hit you with my car. You should be claiming whiplash, spinal injury, threatening to sue. That's what I assumed you were after when you flung yourself in front of my car."

"I didn't fling myself anywhere," she protested.

His dark eyes seemed to trace over her petite, curvaceous body, as if imagining her without her button-up white shirt and khakis. As she blushed, his eyes met hers coolly. "You could be lawyered up, demanding millions."

Millions? That thought hadn't even occurred to Laney. That kind of fortune could have completely changed her life—and more importantly, her family's.

But...

"That wouldn't be right," she said slowly. "I mean,

it wasn't your fault I fell into the street. You did everything you could not to hit me. Your quick reflexes saved my life."

"So if I offered you a million euros right now to sign some kind of legal release attesting to that, you would sign it?"

"No," she said, sadly, cursing her own morals.

His cruelly sensual mouth curved up cynically. "I see—"

"I would sign it for free."

He looked startled. "What?"

"My grandma raised me to tell the truth and not take advantage. Just because you're rich doesn't make me a thief."

Kassius gave a low laugh as he took a tight left turn. "Your grandmother sounds like a remarkable woman."

"She is." She smiled. "A true Southern lady."

Kassius stared at her for a moment, and his dark eyes glimmered in the fading gray twilight.

His car pulled up in front of the grand entrance of the Hôtel de Carillon. But as he turned off the car engine, she saw something in his face that twisted her heart.

Without thinking, she timidly touched his shoulder. She immediately regretted it as she felt the hard muscle beneath his sleek black jacket. Her hand fell away, but she couldn't stop herself from saying, "Why do you look like that?"

His dark eyes met hers. "Like what?"

She wondered if he'd felt the same sizzle of energy she had when they touched. No. Of course not, that was ridiculous. He was interested only in her employer,

who was beautiful, aristocratic and glamorous—
everything that she, Laney, was not.

She took a deep breath. "You look…sad."

Kassius stared at her for a long moment. Then he
gave her an abrupt, hard smile. "Billionaires don't
get sad. We get even." He turned away. "Come on.
I'll save you from Mimi."

Her own car door suddenly opened. Jacques, the
doorman, looked completely and utterly astonished
to find her returning to the building in a sports car.
He said, "Mademoiselle Laney?"

"Oh, hello," she said with an awkward laugh and—
she feared—a guilty expression. "Um. Monsieur
Black was kind enough to offer me a ride in the rain."

Jacques looked even more shocked when he saw
Kassius, who handed him keys and what looked like
a very large tip with a murmured, "*Merci,*" before
he retrieved the carefully wrapped brand-new fur
from the front of the car, then walked with her into
the lavish lobby.

"Tell me," Kassius said casually as they walked,
"What do you think of Mimi? Is she a good employer?"

Laney bit her lip, struggling for words. "I'm grateful for the job," she said finally, with complete honesty. "She pays a generous salary, and I'm supporting
family back home. Thank you for helping me keep it."

But she felt a little less happy about that prospect
from the moment she got back into the comtesse's
suite.

"Laney! You lazy girl! What took you so long?
You wouldn't even answer your phone," her boss said
accusingly the moment she walked in. "You took so

long that I was actually forced to get my own coffee. I had to call room service myself. *Myself!*"

"I'm sorry," Laney stammered. "I was in an accident, and my phone was—"

"Why do I even bother to pay you, you useless—"

Then Mimi saw Kassius enter the suite behind Laney, and her jaw dropped. Her friend Araminta, lounging on the sofa by the windows, smoking and thumbing idly through a *Paris Match*, was so shocked her cigarette fell from her mouth.

Both women instantly rose to their feet, tossing their long hair and tilting their hips.

"Kassius!" Mimi cooed, smiling as if butter wouldn't melt in her mouth. "I didn't realize you were coming for a visit."

"I wasn't. I ran into your assistant on the street."

He winked at Laney, who blushed.

"What do you mean?" The comtesse looked between them, clearly unwilling to be left out of any private joke. Kassius looked irritated.

"I ran into her with my car," he said bluntly.

She whirled on Laney.

"Stupid girl, why did you run out in front of Mr. Black's car?"

Kassius choked out a cough. "It was my fault entirely." He placed the black zipper bag from the expensive furrier into her arms. "Here. To replace your coat that was ruined in the accident."

Zipping it open, Mimi gasped. "A new fur! I take it back, Laney," she said sweetly. "You can let Mr. Black hit you with his car any time he wants."

And Laney didn't think her boss was joking, either.

Mimi's red lips lifted in a flirtatious smile as she

stepped closer to Kassius. "Buying me a new fur coat before we've even gone on our first date? You really know how to please a woman."

"Do you think so?" Kassius glanced sideways at Laney. "It's been a long time since I've been inspired to pursue anyone."

Laney's heart pounded strangely. He couldn't be talking about her—could he? No, of course not. It was her boss he wanted, with all her blonde, slender, wickedly fashionable glory. Not Laney, dumpy, plain, ordinary. And clumsy—so clumsy!

"Just wait until you see me at the ball tonight." Mimi preened. "You'll be inspired to try a few other things to get my attention, maybe like…" Leaning up on her tiptoes, she whispered something in his ear. His expression was unreadable as he drew back from her.

"What an…intriguing thought." He looked around at the three women. "So I will see you tonight?" His gaze paused on Laney. "All of you?"

"Of course Laney's going," the comtesse said. "I need her there holding my handbag with my lipstick and safety pins in case my dress breaks…it's tight and mini and held together by tiny straps." She giggled. "You'll die."

Kassius turned to Laney gravely. "Are you, also, planning to wear such a dress?"

Laney blushed in confusion. "I…that is…"

"Laney?" Her boss laughed. "She'll be wearing a uniform, like the other servants. That's right and proper. Isn't it, Araminta?"

"Right and proper," her friend agreed, lighting a fresh cigarette.

"You should go, Kassius." Mimi waved her hand airily. "Let us get ready for the ball. Laney has a lot to do..."

Kassius turned the full force of his dark gaze on her. "I wondered if you would do me a small favor."

"Anything," she breathed.

Kassius glanced back at Laney. "Laney wouldn't go to a hospital, but she should at least rest. She hit her head. I'm concerned about her. She's seemed a little...out of it."

"Laney's always out of it," Mimi replied irritably, and in this case, Laney privately agreed, though it hadn't been the car accident that had made her brain freeze and her body extra clumsy with sensual awareness. It was Kassius. She'd never had any man affect her like this. Or look at her the way he'd looked at her.

"Do me a favor. Give her the next hour or two off to recuperate."

"But I need her to—" But beneath the force of his gaze, her boss sighed grumpily. "All right. Fine."

"Thank you." His gaze went over all of them but seemed to linger on Laney. Then he tipped his head. "Ladies."

The comtesse and Araminta beamed at him as he turned and left through the door. Then her boss's smile dropped.

"All right, Laney. I don't know what you did to get his attention—his pity—but you truly embarrassed yourself, pushing yourself forward! So tacky!"

"So tacky," Araminta agreed.

"Now go steam my dress."

Without the electric distraction of Kassius beside her, with his powerful body towering over her and his dark sensual gaze, Laney suddenly realized she did have a seriously pounding headache. "But you said I could rest a bit—"

"You can rest while you steam my dress."

"And mine."

"Consider it a gift." The comtesse gave her a hard smile. "Pretend you're at the sauna. The day spa. Enjoy yourself."

And oddly, as Laney stood in front of the tiny, fancy gowns—which seemed to be made solely of hooked ribbons—and steamed the wrinkles out, she did enjoy herself. She kept picturing Kassius's dark eyes searching hers, the resonant timbre of his voice, the touch of his hand as he'd helped her out of the car.

Laney stopped, then shook her head. "You're being ridiculous," she told herself out loud. "At midnight, he'll be kissing her—not me!"

She heard the doorbell of the suite ring. Setting down the garment steamer, Laney hurried to answer the door.

A young man was holding a large box. "Delivery."

"*Merci.*" Giving him a tip from her own wallet— her employer was notoriously cheap where tips were concerned—Laney took the big white box, accompanied by an envelope. "Madame la Comtesse, you have—"

Then Laney looked at the name written on the envelope and nearly staggered in shock.

Mademoiselle Laney Henry.

"What is it?" Her boss was suddenly standing beside her. "A delivery for me?"

"Actually..." Laney breathed. "It's for me."

"What?" Her boss snatched up the envelope. "Who

would send you a gift?" She ripped it open and read the message, then staggered back. She glared at Laney with shock in her thin, lovely face. "What did you do?"

"What do you mean?"

She thrust the note at Laney. She looked down at it.

I'm sure you'd look good in any uniform, but consider this instead. Be there before midnight. Kassius

A hot glow like fire suddenly filled her heart, somewhere between triumph and joy. "He sent me a gift?"

"Open it," Mimi ordered.

Laney wished Mimi and Araminta weren't there so that she could just open his present alone and savor it without their glares. But setting the large white box on the table, she lifted the lid.

All three women gasped.

Inside the white box was a sparkling golden gown. It glistened in the light of the suite, strapless, with a sweetheart neckline and wide, voluminous skirts of glittery tulle. Laney lifted a long white glove from the box and suddenly felt like crying. It was a gift fit for a princess. No one had ever given her anything like this in her whole life.

She lifted the gown completely out of the box, holding it up against her body. She barely recognized her own reflection in the gilded mirror, the laughing brown eyes, the way the golden gown set off her creamy skin and dark hair.

"What did you do, throw yourself in front of his

car on purpose?" Her boss glared at her. "You sneaky little gold digger, dazzling him with some poor-helpless-little-woman routine? I *invented* that routine! You think I'll just let you steal him away from right under my nose?"

She stared at Mimi in shock. "No—"

Her boss looked her over sneeringly, from her plain white shirt to baggy khakis to her sensible clogs. Her lip curled. "What could any man possibly see in you?"

"I'm sure he was just trying to be nice," she stammered.

"Trying to make you jealous, Mimi," Araminta said.

"Maybe." She turned back to Laney. "Fine. Wear that dress. Go to the New Year's Eve gala tonight. And if he asks you to dance—" her eyes narrowed "—I want you to accept."

Her? Dance with Kassius Black? In this dress? In spite of herself, Laney swayed deliriously at the thought, nearly hugging herself with happiness.

"Then—" Mimi looked down at her with her red lips curving "—you will tell him you are sick of his attentions and want him to leave you alone. You will insult him until he believes you."

Laney's sweet candy-pink dreams all fled. "No!"

"If you don't, you'll be out of a job." The comtesse tossed her long blond hair, putting her hand on a tight white-jeans-clad hip. "Not only that, but I'll personally make sure no one ever, ever hires you again. So what's your choice?" Looking at Laney's miserable face, her smile widened as she added sweetly, "I thought so."

CHAPTER TWO

Kassius grabbed a crystal flute of champagne from the tray of a passing waiter, sipped it and wrinkled his nose. Too bubbly. Too sweet. He would have preferred a martini, but then, he would have also preferred to spend the evening driving fast on a curvy road, or getting naked in bed with a beautiful woman, rather than being stuck here at some gala, wearing a tuxedo and surrounded by society revelers, many of whom were already tipsy in spite of the fact it was barely ten o'clock.

The party was hosted by royalty, and guests allowed only by exclusive invitation, so it was well attended. The ballroom was in a grand Belle Époque building off the Avenue Princesse Grace, on a peninsula overlooking the bay. Inside, enormous crystal chandeliers hung from high, painted ceilings, sparkling against gilded walls. An orchestra played music that was ponderous and classical and entirely appropriate, and he didn't much like that, either. He would have preferred rock and roll, or pop, or rap, or even the music that had once been his mother's favorite, the blues. But then, his mother had been originally from New Orleans, where the blues were born.

Just like Laney.

Kassius pictured her sweet, pretty face. Her big brown eyes, so straightforward and honest and kind. Strange that he'd barely noticed her before today, or maybe not so strange, the little helpful servant fading invisibly into the wallpaper behind her employer.

But now, that had all changed.

Now she had his full attention.

Since he'd left Mimi's apartment, he'd already had an investigator run a background check on Laney. Born Elaine May Henry, age twenty-five, from a little town outside New Orleans, graduated high school with top honors but skipped college to go straight to work. Her ailing grandmother and disabled father had needed her income, especially since Laney's mother had abandoned them years before.

The thought of that abandonment made prickles tighten down Kassius's neck. He'd been abandoned by a parent, too. His father. And his own sweetly fragile mother, once the sheltered darling of a wealthy family from a far different New Orleans neighborhood than Laney's, had never recovered.

He pushed the memory away, focusing back on the far more pleasant thought of Laney.

After high school, she'd gone to work as a nanny for a professional football player's family. Two years later, she'd become personal assistant to a famous chef who specialized in Cajun cooking, with a chain of restaurants, including one in Paris. It was there that, two years ago, Mimi had offered her a job at a large increase in pay, then brought her to Monaco. Through it all, one thing remained constant: Laney worked constantly and sent everything home to her family.

She was kind. Loyal. She hadn't complained about her boss, even when Kassius had deliberately given her the opportunity. Nor had she lied and given Mimi nonexistent good qualities. When pressed for her opinion, Laney had simply expressed honest gratitude for the generous salary.

And yet, even needing money so badly, she hadn't asked him for a cent after he'd nearly run her over with his car. She'd barely allowed him to replace the fur coat he'd destroyed, and...he suddenly realized he still owed her a phone. She hadn't brought it up, even when she needed money so desperately, while he had so much now he never even thought about it anymore.

Oh, yes. Laney Henry interested him. After just a single afternoon in her company, he'd seen old-fashioned values he'd heard about, values that were truly rare: self-sacrifice. Kindness. Honesty. Generosity. Loyalty.

And more than that.

Her warm nature attracted him, like bright sunshine after a dark frozen winter. Was it something in the gentle lilt of her voice? Her accent, which reminded him of the all too brief happiness of his early childhood?

Or was it something far more earthy than that? Was he roused by the novelty of Laney's petite body and outrageous curves, so different from the tall, stick-thin, cool-to-the-touch mistresses he'd taken over the years, who had left him sexually sated but never quite satisfied?

Whatever it was, he found himself unable to think of anything but her. He found himself hungering for her sunlight and heat and fire. Craving an old-fashioned woman that he could trust—and even control—because of her own good, kindhearted nature. But also desire. Oh, yes.

Interesting.

For so long, he'd planned his revenge. He was so close now, but there was one part of his plan that hadn't yet fallen into place. When he finally destroyed the old man, revealed his true identity and took everything the man cared about—his failing company, his gaudy pink mansion on Cap Ferrat—Kassius had thought he would already have his own snug home, wife, children. How else could he give the widowed, childless old man one last taunt, by showing him the family he would never see again and the grandchildren who would never have the chance to love him?

Kassius allowed himself a cold smile. Across the ballroom, he could see the old Russian's gray hair as he spoke with friends. Kassius kept his distance, like a shark observing his prey before he went in for the kill.

He suddenly remembered Laney's quiet voice. *You look sad.*

And his own grim reply. *Billionaires don't get sad. We get even.*

Strange that Laney knew what it was like to be abandoned by a parent, too. Kassius had been astonished to read that in the report. But it had affected her very differently. Rather than creating impenetrable armor to protect herself, rather than growing hard and defensive, she'd somehow stayed soft, like a flower. Laney gave the world everything she had and held nothing in reserve.

He wondered what it would be like to kiss her. To do more than kiss her.

He wondered what it would be like to have her petite, curvaceous body in his arms. To have her look up at him with shining brown eyes and tell him, with a sweet tremble in her husky voice, that she wanted him to take her. That she never wanted to leave him. That she was pregnant with his baby.

The image shouldn't have turned him on, but it did. A lot.

In the past, he'd never let himself be vulnerable. Becoming too intimate with any woman might allow her to discover the truth of his past, and his real identity, potentially jeopardizing his plans.

Plus, all the women of his acquaintance were like Mimi du Plessis—beautiful, venal, hard as nails. Mimi would betray anyone for the slightest advantage. Or even, he thought, for her own amusement on a cloudy day.

But then, that was exactly why he'd sought her out.

For nearly twenty years, Kassius had plotted his revenge, rising from poverty on the streets of Istanbul, working night and day with one ruthless goal: to destroy Boris Kuznetsov.

But even Mimi, dim-witted and self-centered as she was, had started to grow suspicious about Kassius gathering up the man's loans and anonymously offering more. They were loans the Russian couldn't hope to repay. The man was desperate to save his flailing energy company and keep providing for his employees. Even useless ones like Mimi, who was supposedly Kuznetsov Oil's director of public relations and corporate outreach, but rarely roused herself to do more than attend cocktail parties.

So Kassius had deliberately let her believe he might be pursuing her. He didn't feel guilty. Mimi du Plessis was well versed in this game, and usually the victor, leaving a trail of broken hearts. She risked only her vanity, not her heart.

But sooner or later, the deception would end. That afternoon, when Mimi had whispered in his ear that she wanted him to handcuff her to a bed and cover her in whipped cream, he'd barely managed to control his revulsion. He wasn't attracted to Mimi at all. If he handcuffed her to a bed, it would be only so he could leave her more swiftly.

But where was she? Why hadn't she arrived yet with Laney?

He wanted to see Laney in the gold dress. Coming out of the elevator, he'd seen the gown in the window of the designer boutique on the first floor of the hotel and impulsively bought it for her. Would it fit? Would she wear it? Would it show off those curves barely hinted at in her shapeless white shirt and oversize khaki pants?

Finishing his champagne, Kassius dropped the flute on a passing silver tray and, giving a wide berth to Boris Kuznetsov, he went in search of a martini—and Laney Henry.

He pushed through the well-heeled crowds on the edge of the enormous dance floor, ignoring the inviting smiles of the women and annoyed glares of lesser men. Walking toward the bar, he looked right and left for the glitter of a gold dress.

Then he saw her.

He stopped. Her big brown eyes widened when she saw him. She stopped, too, and as her delectable lips formed his name, all thought of a martini fled his mind.

He'd known Laney would be beautiful.

He'd never imagined this.

The exquisite golden ball gown showed off her hourglass shape, her full breasts and tiny waist. Her skin looked like creamy caramel, with her long dark hair pulled back in a classic chignon. Her long white gloves reached up past her elbows, so the only bare skin revealed was her upper arms, her shoulders and clavicle, with just an enticing hint of cleavage. She was beautiful to him, as fantastical as a princess from a fairy tale.

And so much more alluring than the skinny, hard-eyed blonde now stepping between them, in a tight, short dress made of strategically placed straps that left almost nothing to the imagination.

"Kassius! Darling! I'm so happy to see you." Mimi du Plessis fluttered her fake eyelashes, then, glancing behind her dismissively, gave a fake, tinkly laugh. "You were so kind to send a dress to my assistant. She might have worn overalls otherwise—no fashion sense whatsoever. Laney." Wrapping her arm around Kassius's shoulder, Mimi squashed her cheek to his as she turned around to face Laney. "Take a picture of us," she demanded, "so we can show everyone what a good time we're having."

But as Laney obligingly lifted her boss's crystal-encrusted phone, Kassius detangled himself before she could take a photo. "Thank you, Mimi, but I prefer my privacy."

She narrowed her eyes. "It's strange, Kassius. You have no online presence. Searching for you on the internet, one comes up with almost nothing."

"Tragic, but then, I'm in real estate development, not the entertainment business," he drawled. His expression changed as he turned to face Laney. "You look beautiful."

"Thank you," she breathed, tilting back her head to meet his gaze. Her dark eyes were wide, her cheeks rosy. "You were so nice to send this dress—what possessed you?"

"You," he said, taking the phone from her and dropping it into Mimi's hands. "Dance with me."

"Dance?" With a troubled glance at her employer, Laney licked her full, pink, delectable lips. Just at that, his body tightened with instantaneous reaction. He nearly groaned aloud. "I don't know if that's a good idea…"

"It's a very good idea," Mimi said smugly. He was almost surprised she was being so reasonable.

"Come now," he said firmly. Taking Laney's gloved hand, he pulled her out onto the marble dance floor, and with a twirl of her skirts, tugged her back hard against his body.

He felt her petite form cradled against him, all soft, lush curves beneath the sparkling gold bodice and wide sweep of skirts. Her skin was bare above her gloves. He had to fight the desire to caress her shoulders, to see if her skin was smooth and satiny as it looked.

"I don't know how to waltz," she confessed, trembling as she lifted her gloved hands to his shoulders.

"It's easy." He gave her a sensual smile. "I will show you what to do."

He adjusted one of her hands on his shoulder, and took the other in his own.

"See?" he murmured. "You're a natural."

Her lips parted as she looked up at him, so pretty, so gentle, so everything he hadn't realized he desperately desired until this exact moment.

Yes, his body said. *Yes. Yes.*

Holding her at the prescribed distance as he led her in a waltz, dancing in time with all the other couples on the ballroom floor, his body hungered. He wanted to get her alone, rip off her clothes and feel her naked body against his. He wanted to be above her. Beneath her. Inside her.

He wanted her in his bed. Tonight. Within the hour. If not sooner.

"Mr. Black…" Laney said falteringly.

"I told you. Kassius."

"Kassius." Her lips trembled as she whispered his name. Looking up at him, she tried to smile politely, but as her fingers tightened, he knew that she felt the same overwhelming current between them.

"You've done so much for me already," she said shyly. "Replacing the fur coat. Defending me to the comtesse." She looked down at her gold ball gown. "But this takes the cake. I've never owned anything half so beautiful as this."

"It made me think of you." He slowly looked her over. "But seeing you in it now, the gown barely does you justice. You are the star."

As they continued to swirl around the dance floor, he saw Mimi glowering at them. She'd already grown suspicious about his loans. One word to her employer and she could make it much harder for Kassius to achieve his goal. If he were smart, he knew he wouldn't pursue Laney like this, flaunting his desire before the other woman's eyes, injuring her pride.

But he couldn't stop himself. After twenty years of obsessive focus on one goal, he found he could no more pull away from this intoxicatingly beautiful, warmhearted woman than he could voluntarily stop breathing.

A blush burned Laney's cheeks as her dark eyelashes swept against her skin. "No one has ever said such…" Then she followed his gaze to Mimi, and her expression shuttered. "Oh," she said, and the sound was like a wistful sigh. "You really are just trying to make her jealous, aren't you?" She shook her head and tried to smile, but her eyes seemed to glimmer. "The games rich people play. You should just try being honest." She abruptly stopped dancing. "Go ask her to dance. And leave me out of it—"

But as she tried to pull away, he held her fast.

"I do not play those kinds of games. I do not need to play them."

"Then why—"

His eyes flicked toward Mimi du Plessis, in her ridiculously tight bandage minidress, whispering to her friend Araminta. "If I wanted her in my bed, she'd already be flat on her back."

"That's a crude thing to say."

"You said you wanted honesty."

"It's not nice."

"I could have her." He slowly looked around the dance floor. "I could have most of these women.

I know, because I have already had some of them, and the rest have made the invitation clear."

"Is this your idea of bragging? Telling me you've slept around? I'm not impressed that you've had so many lovers."

"No?" His hands tightened on her. "But I am impressed you've had so few."

He heard her intake of breath as her eyes widened. "How can you—"

She cut herself off.

"How can I tell?" He ran one hand down her back. "I can tell in the way you shiver when I touch you." He cupped her cheek with the other. "I can tell in the way you hold your breath when I look at you." He twirled her on the dance floor, then pulled her tight against his body. "I can feel it," he said roughly, "in the way your body trembles against mine."

Kassius looked down at her. She was so tiny in his arms, he thought, so feminine and vulnerable. And yet it was her vulnerability that most impressed him. He marveled that anyone could be so fearless.

"It's part of what makes you different," he said in a low voice. "Your warmth. Your kindness. You're not just beautiful. You give so much of yourself and ask for so little."

"I'm…just…ordinary," she said softly, her dark eyes pleading.

"No." He shook his head with a slow-rising smile. "You're far from that."

"You're wrong—"

"You refused to take my money, even when I offered it. Refused to speak badly of Mimi, even though she cannot be a considerate employer. You give up

your whole life to work, to take care of your family."
He ran his hands gently over the nape of her neck.
He yearned to pull her hair out of the prim fastenings
of her chignon and let it tumble down her shoulders.
Abruptly the fantasy came into his mind of her sitting naked on him, her thighs wide, leaning over to
kiss him, long dark hair brushing against his skin as
her full breasts pressed against his chest.

Soon. Soon.

With a deep breath, he took hold of himself and
continued frankly, "Tonight you look like a princess.
But I'm starting to believe it only reflects the way
you are inside. There's something about you I can't
resist…" Leaning forward, allowing his lips to brush
against the sensitive flesh of her ear, he whispered,
"I want you."

But as he drew back and looked down at her, a
shadow crossed her lovely face. With a small glance
back toward her boss, she pulled away from him, her
expression sorrowful.

"I'm sorry, but I'm just not interested."

Kassius hadn't expected that at all, not with the
way he'd felt her trembling in his arms. Had he misjudged her desire?

Then he looked more closely at her beautiful face,
at how she'd turned pale beneath the blush on her
cheeks, her eyes haunted and black. She was lying.
But why?

"Really," he said evenly.

She nodded furiously, but as the couples around
them continued to waltz around where they stood
stock-still on the dance floor, she refused to meet
his gaze.

"Tell me why."

"Because…" She licked her lips uncertainly then lifted her chin. "Because you're a playboy who sleeps around in such a disgusting way."

"Try harder."

"You're not even slightly attractive to me."

"Explain."

She looked him over desperately. "You're too—um—tall."

He snorted. "Too tall?"

"Fine. I'll give you a reason," she snapped. "It's not you, it's me. I'm just a frigid virgin, all right?"

"The virgin I might believe. But frigid?" Shaking his head, Kassius gave a low laugh. Pulling her closer, he ran his hands over her soft, bare shoulders. He felt her tremble as she looked up at him breathlessly. He could see the shape of her taut nipples through her silky bodice. Running his hands slowly, sensuously, down her arms, he said, "You are far from that."

She looked at him with big eyes. "Please…please don't."

"Why?"

"Because—" She swallowed, then said in a voice so low he had to strain to hear, "If I don't make you stop pursuing me, my boss says I'm fired. And she'll make sure I never get another job."

He was so shocked he almost laughed. "She said what?"

But it was obvious Laney didn't see it as a joke but a real threat. Her face was anguished. "If I can't work, how will I support my family? So you have to go away and leave me alone." Her pleading brown gaze fell to his lips as she whispered, "Just go…"

Her words might be saying one thing, but her body was saying another. She didn't even know what she was really asking him for. But he did.

Laney was a virgin? He could hardly believe it. He'd never made love to a virgin before. It was almost cruel. It made him desire her even more, when he was already nearly exploding with need, and would also force him to seduce her more slowly. He didn't know how much more self-restraint he could endure. Where women were concerned, he wasn't accustomed to it.

The orchestra's music stopped, and as the other couples left the dance floor, he felt their curious glances as they passed, felt Mimi's glower from the crowd.

He knew he was making a mistake. He'd always been private to the point of mania, but here, in the literal spotlight, he suddenly didn't care who might be watching.

Pulling Laney roughly against his body, he tangled his hands in her hair, tilting her chin upward. "Get one thing straight," he said, searching her gaze ruthlessly. "I don't give a damn about Mimi or anyone else. I only care about one thing."

She looked at him defiantly. "And what might that be?"

"Taking what I want," he said ruthlessly. "And I want you."

And cupping her face with his hands, he lowered his head and kissed her, right there on the dance floor of the New Year's Eve ball.

His lips were soft against hers at first. Laney felt the roughness of his chin, the sweet taste of his mouth.

She had no idea what to do. The one time she'd been kissed before, it had been a total disaster.

But this was different. *He* was different. As Kassius's mouth began to move more forcefully against hers, taking rather than asking, she realized she didn't have to do anything but surrender. Her eyes squeezed shut.

As she relaxed against him, his kiss deepened, and he pushed her lips apart, plundering her mouth. She nearly gasped at the pleasure that went through her, a *whoosh* of sensation that electrified her from her lips to her earlobes to her breasts and lower still. Her nipples tightened. Low in her belly, she felt a new sensation coil deep inside her.

Pleasure seemed to be exploding from her body like light. She'd never experienced anything like this—never—

"You're mine," he whispered roughly against her lips. "Mine."

She realized she'd tightened her hands against his shoulders, bringing him down hard against her in the kiss. Then he abruptly pulled away, leaving her bereft.

Her eyes flew open, and she saw the orchestra had taken a break—they were alone on the dance floor and the entire ballroom had fallen silent, staring at them. Mimi's eyes were beaming such lasers of fury Laney feared she might burst into flame. Then she remembered.

"Oh, no," Laney choked out. Her hands went to her face in dismay. What had she done, letting him kiss her? How could she have been so selfish as to give in to the moment when her family was counting on her? "What have I done?"

"Nothing. Yet." He sounded almost amused as his larger hand took hers. His dark eyes seared her. "But you will. You're coming home with me. Now."

Laney looked up at him, feeling like her whole future was hanging in the balance.

She looked at Kassius in his sleek bespoke tuxedo, so tall and broad shouldered. Power and wealth clung to him as ineffably as his faint scent of cypress and musk.

There was no way a handsome billionaire could actually want Laney. She was just a regular girl. She liked fried chicken and po' boy sandwiches, not foie gras and caviar. She drank sweet tea, not Dom Pérignon. She bought her clothes from discount warehouses, not based on prestige or even appearance, but comfort and practicality.

She had nothing in common with the typical girlfriends of billionaires—nothing!

"You can't want me. You can't possibly want me."

"Why?" he demanded.

"Why? Because you're—you. And I'm me." She could still hardly believe that she was even here, in this illustrious gilded ballroom in Monaco, with its soaring crystal chandeliers, full orchestra and a thousand members of the international jet set. Her only other dance experience had been at senior prom, in a school gymnasium with paper decorations and balloons, a punch bowl and a DJ. She'd been hopeful and excited, wondering if the high school quarterback would kiss her. And look how *that* night had turned out. "Please just let me go."

Kassius's dark eyes glittered. "Is that really what you want?"

No. No. Of course it wasn't. She felt intoxicated and alive for the first time in her life. She wanted to be beautiful and desired by the most handsome, powerful man on earth, one of the richest men in the world. The thought was like a dream to her. A deliriously impossible dream.

She felt everyone staring at them, the only ones left on the dance floor. The center of attention.

She whispered, "Everyone is staring at us."

"Staring at *you*. They're wondering who you are."

She gave a low laugh. "I've lived here almost two years!"

"As a servant. Invisible." He stroked her bare shoulder, looking down at her in the shimmering gold gown. "You're not invisible anymore."

Because of you, she thought. Her heart was pounding in her throat.

"Come with me. Now. Tonight." His handsome face was hungry and hard as he took her hand.

She did not—could not—resist. He led her through the ballroom, and a path magically cleared for him—all six foot four, two hundred pounds of muscle—through the crowd.

Out of the corner of her eye, she saw Mimi and Araminta's thin, shocked faces as they passed by. But she couldn't think about that now, or her future. All she could do was follow where Kassius led, out of the ballroom and the vast building to the street outside, where a sleek dark car swiftly pulled up to the curb and a uniformed driver hastened to open her door.

Outside, the moon was pearlescent in the dark sky. A ghostlike glow frosted the palm trees swaying in the abrupt hard wind. Winter in Monaco was gener-

ally sunny and mild, but sometimes after a rain, the strange rare wind of the mistral would rise, a legendarily violent wind capable of driving men and women mad.

The mistral. It was her only excuse…

Without a word, Kassius pushed her into the backseat of his limo. The door was barely closed behind them, the vehicle just starting to pull out into the street, before Kassius's mouth was on hers. He pushed her back against the smooth leather, and she closed her eyes, feeling his hands everywhere, over the sparkling layers of her golden gown. His hands ran over her naked shoulders, cupping her face as he kissed her roughly, his mouth searing hers, taking possession without permission or apology. She felt the strength and weight of his body pressing against her.

As he kissed her, he peeled off her long gloves one by one, and as she felt the soft whisper of fabric move slowly down her skin, she shivered from sensation. Her breasts felt heavy beneath the fabric of her strapless bodice, her nipples agonizingly tight and so sensitive as he brushed against her, pushing her beneath him, caressing her, mastering her. She felt bewildered, dizzy.

The passenger door of the limousine suddenly fell open.

She opened her eyes in shock to see that the car was now parked in front of the Hôtel de Carillon. In the heat of their embrace, she hadn't noticed the drive, the route, even Kassius's driver and bodyguard sitting at the front. Both of those men were now standing on the sidewalk beside the open door, carefully not looking in their direction.

REQUEST YOUR FREE BOOKS!

HARLEQUIN

Presents

2 FREE NOVELS PLUS
2 FREE GIFTS!

YES! Please send me 2 FREE Harlequin Presents® novels and my 2 FREE gifts (gifts are worth about $10). After receiving them, if I don't wish to receive any more books, I can return the shipping statement marked "cancel." If I don't cancel, I will receive 6 brand-new novels every month and be billed just $4.30 per book in the U.S. or $5.24 per book in Canada. That's a saving of at least 13% off the cover price! It's quite a bargain! Shipping and handling is just 50¢ per book in the U.S. and 75¢ per book in Canada.* I understand that accepting the 2 free books and gifts places me under no obligation to buy anything. I can always return a shipment and cancel at any time. Even if I never buy another book, the two free books and gifts are mine to keep forever.

106/306 HDN GHRP

Name _____ (PLEASE PRINT)

Address _____ Apt. #

City _____ State/Prov. _____ Zip/Postal Code

Signature (if under 18, a parent or guardian must sign)

Mail to the **Reader Service:**
IN U.S.A.: P.O. Box 1867, Buffalo, NY 14240-1867
IN CANADA: P.O. Box 609, Fort Erie, Ontario L2A 5X3

**Are you a current subscriber to Harlequin Presents® books
and want to receive the larger-print edition?
Call 1-800-873-8635 or visit www.ReaderService.com.**

* Terms and prices subject to change without notice. Prices do not include applicable taxes. Sales tax applicable in N.Y. Canadian residents will be charged applicable taxes. Offer not valid in Quebec. This offer is limited to one order per household. Not valid for current subscribers to Harlequin Presents books. All orders subject to credit approval. Credit or debit balances in a customer's account(s) may be offset by any other outstanding balance owed by or to the customer. Please allow 4 to 6 weeks for delivery. Offer available while quantities last.

Your Privacy—The Reader Service is committed to protecting your privacy. Our Privacy Policy is available online at www.ReaderService.com or upon request from the Reader Service.

We make a portion of our mailing list available to reputable third parties that offer products we believe may interest you. If you prefer that we not exchange your name with third parties, or if you wish to clarify or modify your communication preferences, please visit us at www.ReaderService.com/consumerchoice or write to us at Reader Service Preference Service, P.O. Box 9062, Buffalo, NY 14240-9062. Include your complete name and address.

HPI5

JUST CAN'T GET ENOUGH
OF THE ALPHA MALE?
Us either!

Come join us at **I Heart Presents** to hear the
latest from your favorite Harlequin Presents
authors and get special behind-the-scenes secrets
of the Presents team!

With access to the latest breaking news and
special promotions, **I Heart Presents** is *the*
destination for all things Presents. Get up close
and personal with the sexy alpha heroes who
make your heart beat faster and share your love
of these glitzy, glamorous reads with the authors,
the editors and fellow Presents fans!

The doorman, Jacques, had no such discretion. When he came forward, his mouth fell open.

"Mademoiselle Laney?"

Her cheeks went hot with shame as she sat up hurriedly, making sure her breasts weren't falling out of the bodice of her dress. She could only imagine what she looked like...

"Thank you," Kassius said coolly, "but I'll help her out." Getting out of the limo, he turned and held out his hand. With a deep breath, feeling overwhelmed with embarrassment and humiliation, she tried to keep her face expressionless as he led her past the doorman into the lobby of the residential hotel.

"You're bringing me home," she whispered over the lump in her throat. She wasn't even surprised. She could still hear that harsh voice from long ago. *Frigid little virgin...*

"Yes," Kassius said.

"You brought me home before midnight." She gave him a weak smile. "Like Cinderella."

They reached the elevator, and the doors opened. He drew her inside and pushed the button.

"That's the wrong floor. Mimi doesn't live in the penthouse."

"But I do."

Her heart twisted in her chest.

"You do?" she whispered.

He came closer to her in the elevator, looking down at her. He cupped her cheek. "I just bought it."

"You did?" She looked up at him, feeling dizzy and strange. "Why?"

"I needed a place in Monaco." His voice was

husky. Sexy. "Until I am able to buy a special villa I want on Cap Ferrat."

"You—you want me to come upstairs with you?" she breathed, hardly knowing what she was saying.

"I do," he whispered, running his hand down the side of her neck. The edges of his lips curved upward. "And you will…"

Roughly, he pushed her back against the mirrored elevator wall. Her head fell back as she closed her eyes, lost in sensation as he kissed down her neck, her cheek, sucking her earlobe as his hands ran over her bare arms, her shoulders, cupping her breasts through the fabric.

The elevator door opened to the top floor, and for a minute she didn't, *couldn't*, move, just leaned back against the mirror, her knees feeling weak.

So he picked her up as if she weighed nothing. Her sparkly tulle skirts fluttered behind them as he carried her swiftly down the hall.

Held against his powerful chest, Laney looked up at him in a daze as he brought her into the luxurious penthouse suite of the Hôtel de Carillon.

The suite was dark, but she could see the ceilings were two stories high. The furniture was stark and modern, but she barely saw it amid the shadows before her gaze was transfixed by the wall of floor-to-ceiling windows with views of the sparkling lights of nighttime Monaco, and beyond that, the vast dark Mediterranean.

Kassius set her down slowly, letting her body drag against his, falling in a cascade of tulle. For a moment, he looked down at her, then with a low growl, he whirled her around so he was looking at her back.

She blinked at the view. She saw a few lights of ships floating through the dark sea, like stars in the sky.

She shouldn't be here. She should go. But she felt like time and reality had fled, as if she were someone else entirely. Someone reckless...

He slowly unzipped her dress, dropping it to the floor. The cool air licked at her skin as he turned her back around to face him. She was almost naked, wearing only a strapless white bra and plain white lace panties. He slowly looked her over. "You are so beautiful."

And even in the shadows of the penthouse suite, she saw in the hard lines of his face, of his body, that he did desire her. Fiercely.

She should leave. Her brain and heart were begging her to leave—leave now. Because there was only one way this could end. Badly.

But for some reason, her body refused to budge as he pulled off her shoes, one by one.

Rising to his feet, Kassius slipped off his black tuxedo jacket. Taking her hand, he drew her into the bedroom.

Translucent gauze curtains covered the windows and sliding glass door to the balcony. He opened the balcony door, and she took a deep breath of the cool, hard wind, scented of salt sea and golden mimosa flowers in bloom.

Laney stood nearly naked in front of Kassius Black—this handsome, dangerous billionaire who was so much larger than she, in every possible way. She lifted her face to his.

His dark eyes were hungry as he came back toward her, and, nervously, she backed away from him, falling back softly onto his enormous king-size bed, against the large white pillows on the white comforter. Standing over her, he deliberately pulled off his black tie.

Wearing only his white shirt and black tuxedo trousers, he kicked off his shoes and reached toward her on the bed. Slowly, he ran his fingertips down her cheek, then her throat, then the hollow between her breasts. She could not move as his fingertips lightly stroked downward, past her silky strapless white bra to her rib cage and the bare skin of her belly. His hand traced downward, ever downward, to the top edge of her lacy white panties.

She suddenly stopped him with her hand.

"Don't," she choked out.

His forehead furrowed. "Why?"

"I'll only disappoint you."

"You're a virgin. How do you know?"

"I know."

Silvery moonlight streaked through the windows, frosting the gauzy curtains and the hard lines of his cheekbones and jaw as he leaned back, staring down at her incredulously. "You actually think you're frigid, don't you?"

"I know I am."

"Why?"

"The boy who took me to prom…he told me."

"And you believed him?"

"He would know. He kissed a lot of girls." A lump rose in Laney's throat. "Look, it's almost midnight. You should go back to the party. Find someone who knows how to kiss—"

"I have the one I want." His fingertips changed

course, skimming over the curve of her hips to her bare thighs.

"Look—" she swallowed "—I don't know why you chose me, whether you're just slumming or—"

He abruptly dropped his hand.

"You spoke earlier about games, Laney. Let's play a game now, you and I."

"What game?"

His gaze locked with hers. "I will prove to you that you are not frigid. That you are a warm, desirable woman. A woman made for pleasure."

"What if you can't?"

He gave a low laugh. "I will. All I have to do is touch you—even look at you—to know I am right."

"And if you're wrong?" she said desperately, remembering the humiliating night of prom when she was eighteen.

"Then I will pay a forfeit." He smiled. "Shall we say—one million dollars?"

She gaped at him. "Is that a joke?"

"No."

"That's the second time you've offered me a million!"

"Is it not enough?" he said lazily, looking at her beneath heavily lidded eyes. "Two million, then. Ten. I am so sure that I can make you gasp with desire, so sure I can make you explode with pleasure, that if I am wrong, Laney, I will pay you ten million dollars."

A noisy burst of wind flew through the open balcony door.

Ten million dollars.

The amount staggered her. She thought of what it would mean. No more abuse from her horrible boss.

She could go back to New Orleans and hire full-time caregivers for her father. Her grandmother, who'd worked her fingers to the bone for fifty years, could finally relax and enjoy her life. Laney could be with the family she loved.

"But the amount I'll pay if I lose doesn't matter." Kassius looked down at her, his eyes glinting wickedly in the moonlight. "Because I will win."

Laney licked her lips. "Just for the sake of argument, if you do make me, um…if you prove I'm not frigid, then what would you want in return?"

"Beyond the sweet prize of your body?" He moved suddenly, leaning over the bed, running his wide hand in a sensual stroke down her body. His expression was deadly serious. "You would be completely mine."

Her mouth went dry. "What do you mean?"

He ran his hand softly against her cheek. "I am tired of the bachelor life. I want a family. I want a wife. Children."

Now she really did feel dizzy. Could the half a glass of champagne she'd drunk at the party be affecting her brain? "You can't possibly mean—"

"If I cannot give you pleasure, Laney, I will give you ten million dollars and you will walk out of here a wealthy woman. But if I make you explode with joy, you will surrender everything. You will allow me to take possession of your body and fill you with my child. You will be mine—forever."

CHAPTER THREE

LANEY SAT UP straight on the king-size bed, her eyes wide. Before, she'd thought she was dreaming, or possibly drunk.

Now she wondered if she'd lost her mind.

"Let me see if I understand," she said faintly. "If you make me come, I must marry you and have your baby?"

Kassius's expression was unreadable. "What is your answer?"

"It's either a ridiculous joke, or else you're crazy!"

"I'm perfectly sane, and I've never been more serious."

"But risking marriage—children—based on sex? That is insane!" Her eyes went wide as he pulled off his shirt, dropping it to the floor. She stared at his hard, muscular chest, laced with dark hair. She licked her lips and tried to remember what she'd been saying. She stammered, "We'd need to be in love. We'd need to be compatible partners. You have to be sensible—"

Leaning over the bed, he stopped her with a kiss. His lips were hard and hot, his muscled chest pressing against her. She was suddenly very aware she was wearing only a strapless bra and panties.

He drew back, searching her gaze. "Your answer."

No would be the sensible response.

Hell, no would be even smarter, while running out of here like her hair was on fire.

But…

Ten million dollars.

Though inexperienced, Laney knew quite a bit about sex, of course. She'd seen her share of R-rated movies, so it wasn't like she was a total innocent. When Bobby Joe Branford, the football hero of her high school, had asked her to prom, she'd been excited at the thought of her first kiss.

But the night had been a disaster. Halfway through the dance, he'd pushed her out into a dark school hallway and kissed her against the lockers. His lips had been rubbery and cold, and she'd nearly choked when she'd tasted sour whiskey on his breath as his tongue shoved down her throat. It was so horrible she knew she must be doing it wrong. She'd tried to remain perfectly still, until finally she could take no more and she tried to push him away. He wouldn't let her, so she'd given him a hard shove with all her strength. He'd fallen to the floor in drunken surprise just as some of his friends walked by. They'd laughed, and Bobby Joe had glared at her.

"Frigid little virgin." He'd wiped his mouth. "I should have known I'd be wasting my time with you."

Bobby Joe had caught up with his friends and found another girl to dance with, leaving Laney in her wrinkled secondhand prom dress and wilting corsage to find her own way home.

But it had gotten even worse. She'd returned to school Monday to find herself a laughingstock. She'd already been unpopular, the short, chubby girl who lived in that ratty house near the bayou, who wore outdated clothes from the thrift shop, whose blind father was in a wheelchair and whose mother had abandoned her family, to run off to California with her lover.

But now the high school quarterback had rendered final, fatal judgment, and the entire school thought of her in his terms: *frigid little virgin*. The other students didn't just think it, either. They called her that. To her face.

Remembering the bewildering pain and humiliation, Laney still felt hot all over, then deadly cold.

All that pain had to be for something.

What was the risk? She would take that ten million dollars and walk out of here like a queen, able to take care of her family for the rest of her life.

Lifting her chin, she looked at Kassius Black with glittering eyes. "I accept."

A flash of triumph crossed his handsome face. Leaning forward, he loosened the pins of her chignon, causing her long dark hair to tumble down her shoulders.

"At last," he said huskily and pressed her back against the bed, kissing her, hard and deep.

She felt nothing. That ten million dollars was as good as in her pocket.

He ran his hands slowly, softly down her body. His kiss gentled. Where a moment before his lips had demanded and possessed, now they caressed like a whisper. Luring her.

She felt a strange shiver in her breasts and low in her belly. She pushed it away. *Frigid little virgin.*

Moving his hands behind her, he unlatched her strapless white bra. She nearly gasped as her full breasts spilled naked into his hands.

With a soft hiss of appreciation, he pushed her back against the bed, running his hands down her body. He cupped a heavy breast, squeezing it lightly, until the full, ripe pink of her nipple presented itself between his fingers like a rose-colored pearl.

She felt *nothing*, she told herself. Her heart was pounding. She was *like stone*.

He lowered his head. She felt the warmth of his breath, then he pulled her virgin nipple fully into his mouth. As he suckled her, electricity sizzled up and down the length of her body. She stiffened, gripping his shoulders tightly.

Like stone, she told herself desperately. *Stone!*

He cupped her other breast, suckling the taut, red, aching nipple. She sucked in her breath.

Suddenly, he gripped both her wrists, pushing them up against the headboard. Leaning forward, he growled in her ear, "You are going to lose."

"I won't," she panted, but a trickle of fear went down her spine. She couldn't lose. Not only would she lose her family's security, but her own. It would mean possibly getting pregnant by a man she barely knew. Becoming his wife. It would mean a loveless marriage. She wouldn't do that just for one moment of pleasure! She couldn't, wouldn't, let herself do that.

Could she...?

His heavily muscled body pressed hers deeper into the mattress. His hard grip held down her wrists as he kissed her, then licked and nibbled down her throat, her earlobes, her clavicle. She felt the hardness of him, straining between her legs. She whimpered.

Releasing her wrists, he kissed her more gently now, stroking her with his hands, caressing her cheek, her throat, her aching breasts. He explored her belly, the curve of her hips. He ran his fingertips along the top edge of her white cotton panties, teasing her. His touch was like a whisper.

No. Her hands gripped the white comforter beneath her.

She couldn't let herself feel pleasure!

She had to resist!

He paused, then deliberately stroked over the thin cotton panties, over the mound between her legs. She choked back a gasp, biting down hard on her lip. He kept moving downward, running his palms over her thighs, causing prickles of heat to spread across her body.

Pushing her legs apart, he lowered his head in little kisses down her belly, all the way down to where his hands recently had touched. He paused at the top of her panties, then deliberately teased her with the warmth of his breath, kissing the edges of the fabric, stoking her desire.

Desire. Was that what she felt? She desired him. But she couldn't. This couldn't happen.

Getting pregnant would change her life forever. And not just hers. She'd always known when she became a mother, she would do it properly. She'd find a nice, kind, trustworthy man whom she loved. They would date for a year, pay for their own simple wedding with the income from their sensible, stable jobs, then save up for the deposit for a house with a white picket fence. Only then, when they both were ready, would they deliberately choose to bring a child into the world. Because a baby deserved security and love and stability. Laney knew this better than anyone.

So even if the chance was small that she could get pregnant tonight, she couldn't take that risk. Not for some ridiculous challenge!

She had to tell him to stop. To call off this game. Tell him he could keep his stupid money.

She had to get out of here, before it was too late!

Just be stone! Her brain shrieked.

The trouble was she no longer felt like stone.

Her breaths came in little gasps as he knelt at the foot of the bed, between her legs. Noises suddenly thundered outside, in explosions. They both turned to face the windows of the balcony. Through the translucent curtains, they saw brilliant fireworks bursting across the dark sky. Kassius looked down at her.

"It's midnight," he said huskily. "Happy New Year."

Cupping her cheek, he kissed her. His mouth was searing, demanding. She felt the roughness of his chin, felt the lure of his tongue against hers. She was lost in his sensual warmth, held beneath the weight of his powerfully muscled body, and worse—the weight of her own desire.

Just one more minute, and I'll tell him to stop, she promised herself. *Just one more minute…*

A burst of wind swirled the gauzy curtains, filling the room, twisting around their entwined, half-naked bodies and cooling their overheated skin. She clutched at his shoulders.

Holding her down, he pushed her lips firmly apart, stroking her tongue with his own. He lured her, enticed her, until suddenly she realized she was kissing him back. Moments later—or maybe hours—he lifted his head. But she didn't have time to catch her breath as he moved down her body. His soft, wet mouth wrapped around her hard, aching nipple, and pleasure ripped through her.

She swallowed, squeezing her eyes shut, gasping beneath the sensual wet swirl of his mouth. His hands slowly stroked her hips. Her thighs. The tender skin between them.

He straightened from the bed and slowly slid her panties over her thighs, down her legs, before tossing them to the floor.

She was completely naked now, spread-eagle across his enormous bed.

"You—frigid!" he muttered almost angrily. "What fool convinced you of that!"

He dropped his trousers and silk boxers to the floor. He sprang out, thick and hard and unrestrained.

She looked at Kassius's naked, powerful body in the moonlight and couldn't look away.

His chest was muscled like warm marble, and the trail of dark hair went down his body to his flat, taut belly. Beneath that… She swallowed. It was the first time she'd seen a fully naked, erect man. He was huge, both in girth and length, and so hard.

Her hand tentatively reached out. He grabbed it.

"Please, can I?" She took a deep breath. "I've never…" She blushed. "Never touched…"

He stared at her. Then released her hand.

She shyly reached out to touch him lightly with

her fingertips, stroking the edges of his shaft. He felt like velvet over steel. He bucked beneath her stroke.

She looked up at him in shock. "You…want me… so badly?"

"Let me show you," he said huskily.

Placing his hands on her shoulders, he pushed her back against the mattress and kissed her hungrily, covering her with his naked body. She felt the heaviness of his muscled legs, rough with hair, against her own, felt his stubbled jawline like sandpaper against her soft skin. Most of all, she felt the thick hardness of him against her belly.

She was tight and aching all over. She nearly cried out from the friction of his hard chest against her sensitive nipples as he slid down her body. She felt him between her legs, demanding entry, and it was all she could do not to spread her legs wider, like a wanton desperate to have him inside her. But he kept moving down, down, all the way to her feet.

Kneeling between her legs, he kissed the hollow of a foot, and the sensitive back of her knee. He stroked slowly up to his thighs, pushing her thighs farther apart.

"What are you—"

"Shh," he whispered. "You'll like it."

He lowered his head. She felt his hot breath on the tender skin of her inner thighs, and a rush of desperate need coursed through her. She knew she was running out of time. She had to push him away, to tell him no, to jump up and run screaming from the bed.

But she couldn't. She gripped the white comforter, her body shaking, unable to stop him as he lowered his head between her legs.

Reaching his hands around her backside, he held her tight, and she felt the warmth of his breath on her most secret core. For a moment, he paused. As if giving her one last chance to refuse.

Then he ruthlessly lowered his head. Spreading her wide, he took a long, languorous taste with the full roughness of his tongue. As she gasped, he sighed in pleasure.

"You taste like caramel," he whispered huskily. "Salty and sweet."

She felt his hot breath on her thighs as he nuzzled her. Felt the roughness of his bristly chin against her thighs, the silky swirl of his mouth against her aching wet core. Involuntarily, her hips rose to meet the thrust of his mouth...

This was madness. She had to stop now. Now!

Just one more minute, she thought desperately. *Just one.* She would die if she didn't have one more minute...

Her hips twisted beneath his mouth as he worked her with his tongue, swirling around her. He eased a finger just barely inside her. She gasped, gripping the bed. She started to shake.

Pushing the finger inside her, then another, he stretched her even as his satin-steel lips and slick wet tongue worked her, making her hold her breath, giving her pleasure until her toes started to curl and she saw stars behind her eyes.

She couldn't...

Oh, this was so good!

She mustn't...

Don't stop!

As he lapped her with his wide tongue, his thick

fingers inside her, her shaking intensified. Pushing her thighs more roughly apart, he suckled her, twirling her with the tip of his tongue, then lapping her. Her hips twisted beneath him, but he held her tight against his mouth, forcing her to surrender, to accept the pleasure. She gripped his shoulders, and her back started to arch. Her hips rose from the bed as she started to writhe beneath him. Her lips parted as she held her breath…held it and held it and…

Pleasure exploded in patterns of light and color. She cried out, gripping into his shoulders, deep, deep, deep with her fingernails, her dark hair flying in a cloud as she shuddered and shook and gasped for air.

Lifting his mouth off her, he positioned his hips between her legs. He filled her with a single thrust.

She cried out as he ripped ruthlessly through her barrier, impaling her to the hilt, hard and deep. In the middle of blinding pleasure, she felt searing pain.

He didn't move, just held himself still inside her. He took a deep breath, as if steadying himself. Then he lowered his head to her ear. She could hear the masculine smugness, the triumph in his cruel, sensual whisper.

"You're mine now."

Kassius nearly passed out with the sensation of burying himself inside her hot, tight sheath.

She felt so good. Even better than he'd dreamed. Her body was soft and slick with sweat and the loud cry of her pleasure was still ringing in his ears. For a moment, his hard thick length pulsed wildly inside her, and he had to fight to keep himself from exploding right there and then, on the first thrust.

For the last hour, he'd held himself back. He liked to believe he had amazing self-control, but a man could only stand so much.

Kissing Laney, suckling her, feeling her naked body against his own, tasting her—it had been sweet torture. All he'd been able to think about was how desperately he wanted to plunge himself inside her tight body, to fill her with a single thrust. She'd sorely tested his self-restraint as he proved she was a woman made for loving, built for pleasure.

Laney—frigid! He still marveled at the ridiculous idea. He could hardly believe that any man had convinced her of that. But he was almost glad. Now she was his, and his alone. She'd been trembling and warm, a goddess of desire.

He'd never wanted any woman more.

And he wasn't interested in a one-night stand. He didn't want a simple love affair. He didn't want to spend weeks, months, years pursuing her, convincing her of his love.

Kassius was ready to settle down. He wanted a real home, with the pride of a wife and family in addition to the success of his business empire.

But not just any woman would do. He needed a wife he could trust. An old-fashioned woman who would be devoted to their family and home—and obey his every command. All that, and she had to be so delicious in bed that he'd want no other.

He'd found her.

He could have just seduced her, without playing the game or extracting her promise. But he'd wanted Laney Henry to know exactly what he intended to take from her—and what he intended to give. He wanted their relationship sealed without question, starting as he meant to go on. With her full and complete surrender.

She would be his wife. He'd get her pregnant as soon as possible.

A low groan came from him at the thought of Laney, heavily pregnant, buxom and round. As he'd first pushed inside her, filling her deeply with one rough thrust, it was lucky he hadn't immediately exploded inside her like a damned volcano.

Now, so deeply inside her, he held himself very still, holding his breath until he could regain control. Then he looked down at her beautiful face, glorying in the moment of his possession as he said huskily, "You're mine now."

She opened her big brown eyes, and he saw her pain. The ecstasy had disappeared. Instead, her teeth were clenched. *Virgin.* Damn it. He cursed himself silently. He'd been so focused on his previous goal of giving her pleasure, then his desperation to satisfy his own pent-up desire, that he'd forgotten it would be painful for her.

He lowered his head. "I'm sorry," he said in a low voice. "I forgot it can hurt the first time. I've never been with a virgin before."

"Me neither," she whispered and tried to smile.

Cupping her cheek, he lowered his head and kissed her lips gently. He tasted the salt of her tears. He kissed them away. At first, she didn't respond. For long moments, he did not move his hips, just giving her body time to adjust to the feel of him, hard and deep inside her.

Then he heard a sound from her like a sigh, and in

his soft, slow embrace, her shoulders started to relax. Tentatively, she reached up and stroked his chest, which was heavily muscled from his years training as a boxer and martial arts fighter.

He shuddered beneath her soft touch. Pressing his body against hers, he gloried in the sensation of her bare skin against his, the fullness of her breasts crushed against his chest.

She was soft, so soft. He couldn't remember the last time he'd had a woman with a shape like this, so petite and sensual. Had he ever? He doubted it. His taste in lovers had always been conformist—he'd chosen the same tall, super-slender supermodels as every other billionaire, just as he chose the same type of sports car and expensive yacht and palatial ski lodge. In his business empire, he was an innovator. In his personal life, he'd been depressingly unoriginal.

Until now.

Until *her*.

He didn't know how much longer he could keep still. Even after all this time without moving inside her, he was so hard and aching he thought he might burst. Feeling her softly curved body beneath his, so pliable and desirable in every way, he wanted to ride her, hard and fast, until he exploded with joy.

But even that wasn't enough. Part of what had made him so crazy was watching her face as he gave her pleasure for the first time. Ten million dollars had been hanging in the balance, truly an immense fortune to someone with her background, and yet Laney still hadn't been able to hide her own passionate nature, or resist her desire.

Kassius wanted more of that. He wanted to make

her writhe and gasp all over again. To make her reach a level of ecstasy greater than the one before. To hear her cry out his name. Only that would satisfy him now.

He deepened the kiss, and when she kissed him back, wrapping her arms around his shoulders, only then did he start to move inside her, inch by inch, with agonizing slowness that tortured him, when all he wanted to do was slam himself into her.

Instead, he swayed his hips back and forth, gritting his teeth as he held himself on the razor's edge of self-control. Again. Slower. He stroked her.

She gave a soft gasp. He looked down at her beautiful face. Her eyes were squeezed shut with new rapture; her cheeks were rosy and flushed with heat. Her red, bruised lips parted, and he couldn't resist the invitation. Lowering his mouth to hers, he nibbled her lower lip, flicking her with his tongue. As he kissed her, he finally started to increase the pace he thrust inside her, riding her harder, faster.

He felt the quick rise and fall of her breath beneath him, her lusciously full breasts moving against his chest. She writhed and swayed, and her fingernails dug into the flesh of his shoulders. Her whole body clenched beneath him as she held her breath, then suddenly she started to shake; suddenly she was screaming his name. His name...

It was too much. With a low cry, he thrust inside her one last time, so deep, deep, deep, he lost track of where he ended and she began, filling her to the core, and he felt such mind-blowing pleasure that his own low, hoarse shout joined hers as he exploded.

When he opened his eyes again, the moonlight had

shifted slightly across the bed. He looked down, and saw that he was holding Laney's petite body tightly in his arms. Odd. He'd never fallen asleep in a lover's arms.

But he'd never had a night like this. Or a woman like this.

Laney's long dark eyelashes fluttered across her creamy skin, her cheeks still flushed pink from the intensity of their lovemaking as she slept. Kassius felt a strange sense of tenderness as looked down at her, this woman who had fallen in front of his car, the employee of his father's employee, who somehow already wielded such power over him. She didn't realize how much.

And he'd make sure she never would.

She smiled in her dreams, her small body naked and warm in his arms, her long dark hair tumbling over the pillow they shared.

Marveling, Kassius took a deep breath. He was the only man who'd ever had her, and the only one who ever would. He would get her pregnant as soon as possible and make her his bride.

She'd be in his bed every night. The thought made him shiver inside. He intended to take long, hard use of her. She almost made him feel like he, too, was a virgin. As if, even with all his sexual experience, he'd never had the full measure of pleasure. Until her.

He had her now. And he never intended to let her go.

CHAPTER FOUR

THE NEXT MORNING, Laney sighed in satisfaction as she rinsed shampoo from her hair. She yawned, stretching in the hot, steamy shower. She felt like she'd barely slept, but her whole body ached with happiness, every muscle, every sinew, especially the secret places Kassius had explored last night. She'd woken up glowing with happiness after a night in his bed, sleeping in his arms. She'd only woken when he'd stirred beside her when his phone rang. Some business call from a distant place. She'd felt grimy, so as he took the call, she'd stumbled into the shower.

Now, standing in the enormous white marble bathroom of the penthouse, it was hard not to linger over the memory of the lovemaking that had caused all that sweat on her skin. As she washed away the traces of his many kisses, the sweet ache of her well-used body remained. She shivered, no longer just warmed by the steamy water but by the memory of how ruthlessly he'd taken her virginity.

Then she straightened beneath the hot water, as *everything* she'd done last night reasserted itself in her memory. Including the fact that they'd made love with no protection whatsoever.

What the hell had she been thinking?

"Oh, no," Laney whispered. Closing her eyes, she leaned her forehead against the cool tile.

She was a good girl who'd always followed the rules. She knew the potential ramifications of getting pregnant—how could she not? Her parents, high school sweethearts, had already broken up before her mother discovered she was pregnant. Her father had done the dutiful thing and married her, only to discover that they couldn't live together without loud arguments. He'd promptly found work on an oil rig that required long months away in the Gulf of Mexico—it paid well, plus he got time away from his wife. The marriage had bumbled along until Laney was ten, when her father was in a horrific accident on the rig, which caused him to lose his sight and the ability to walk. When his broken body was returned to New Orleans, it was the last straw for her mother.

Rhonda Henry had announced she'd had enough of sacrificing herself for other people. Dumping her husband and child on her mother-in-law's doorstep, Rhonda had hitched a ride with her musician boyfriend, heading west for love, fame and fortune in California. But love swiftly disappeared, and fame and fortune never came. Her mother had comforted her disappointment at first with alcohol, then worse things, until years later she'd died of an overdose on a beach near the Santa Monica Pier.

It had all started with Rhonda accidentally getting pregnant. If not for that, maybe her mother would be alive now, and her father strong and unhurt. If not for Laney being born.

Now she'd taken such a risk!

Stupid. So stupid. She covered her face with her hands. How could she have done it?

Especially knowing that she was certainly going to get fired today?

Turning off the water abruptly, Laney got out of the shower and wrapped herself in a towel.

She wiped the steam off the mirror. Her chin lifted as she looked at the reflection of her own dark, haunted eyes, at her wet hair that looked black cascading down her shoulders.

Whatever Kassius had said last night in the heat of the moment, fairy tales didn't come true. Princes didn't marry housemaids. Handsome billionaires didn't marry ordinary-looking personal assistants.

She would just have to go home and figure it out.

Home. A lump rose in Laney's throat as she thought of her father and grandmother. It had been two years since she'd seen them. She'd been away for too long, trying to earn enough money to support them all. But without her job here in Monaco, how would they all survive?

Taking a deep breath, she started to comb her wet hair. She'd just have to be strong, that was all. Maybe she'd get lucky. Maybe she could talk to Mimi. Convince her to forgive.

Yeah, right.

She reached for the oversize white robe on the back of the door. Kassius's robe? It hung huge on her, dragging on the floor, making her feel like a child dressed up in grown-up clothes. The sleeves hung well over her hands. She rolled them up, then pulled the belt as tightly around her as she could before she went to the kitchen.

"Good morning." Kassius looked at her appreciatively. "I like you in that."

Her cheeks colored. "Thanks. Is that coffee?"

He gave her a sudden grin. "Made it myself."

"Really?" she said, musing how the comtesse wouldn't have known how to pour water from the tap. "Yourself?"

"It's New Year's. My housekeeper has the day off. I'm not totally incompetent. I can make coffee, eggs and toast."

"Wow."

"No sarcasm, please. Not until you taste this." Pouring her a cup, he said, "Cream or sugar?"

"Both, please."

He added two lumps of sugar and a good amount of cream then watched her as she drank it.

"Good?"

Her whole body relaxed with a sigh. She said honestly, "The best coffee I've ever had."

"I thought so," he said smugly. "Now go sit down."

A moment later, he brought out two plates with buttered toast and scrambled eggs. Sliding a plate in front of her, placed his own across from her at the dining table.

She took a bite of the food and was astonished.

"This is delicious."

"Of course it is. I'm good at everything."

"Modest, too."

He took a bite of toast. "You're pretty good yourself." Their eyes met across the table. "I've never met a sexier woman in my life."

That reminded her. She bit her lip unhappily. "Last night, we had sex…without protection."

"Yes," he agreed, taking a bite of scrambled eggs. He didn't look at all sorry about it.

"Was I drunk? Were you?" She put down her fork. "To risk getting pregnant by someone I barely know…"

"If you feel you'd like to know me a little better—" his gaze fell to her breasts, then he gave her a smoldering smile "—we could go back to bed."

Her cheeks went hot as she looked down and saw the top of the oversize robe was gaping widely, showing far more of her chest than was decent. She yanked the robe up higher. "How can you joke?"

His expression changed. "Joke?"

"I can't believe I risked getting pregnant when I'm about to be unemployed!" She clawed back her wet dark hair, blinking back tears as she raged, "How could I have been so stupid!"

He looked at her skeptically. "Are you seriously worried about losing your job? You can't tell me you'll miss Mimi."

"No, but—"

"You have nothing to worry about." His voice was distinctly chilly as he abruptly rose from the table. "I'll go with you to Mimi's."

"You will?" Hope suddenly rose in her. "You'll talk to her? Try to convince her to keep me on?"

"No. It's better to end this quickly."

Better to end this quickly. Her hope faded, and she felt a little sick inside. Bad enough that she'd slept with him without protection. But would she now discover he'd just been slumming with a one-night stand and had taken her virginity as a momentary amusement? Had all his talk about marriage and children been a lie, or a whim, already forgotten?

Kassius being who he was, and Laney being— well, who she was—how could it be otherwise?

Hiding her deep hurt and regret, she looked down at the white robe. "What should I wear? This?" She lifted her arm, with the oversize sleeve hanging past her hand, to point at the gold ball gown still crumpled on the floor from the night before. "Or that?"

His sensual lips quirked. "You pick."

She sighed, then grumbled, "Robe, I guess." Finishing the coffee and food, she said sullenly, "Thanks for breakfast."

"My pleasure."

As she rose to leave, he followed her. She turned to him, desperate for the awkwardness to end. "You don't need to walk me down. There's really no need."

"Oh, but there is." He shrugged. "Anyway, I need to talk to Mimi."

Now he was done taking her virginity, did he want to make romantic plans with her soon-to-be-former boss? Laney's scowl deepened. "Fine."

Silence fell as they got in the elevator and pressed the button for her boss's floor. She couldn't help comparing this ghastly morning-after situation to last night, when they'd steamed up the mirrors, unable to keep their hands off each other.

She glanced at him out of the corner of her eye. Even now, when she was horrified and furious at herself, she could understand why, after being sensible and quiet her whole life, she hadn't been able to resist him. Kassius had made her feel beautiful. Desired.

She'd been swallowed up by ecstasy, devoured by the pleasure of the moment.

But now the moment was over. As soon as she was fired and had packed her things, she'd return to New Orleans. Soon, this night—the most amazing night of her life—would be nothing more than a distant memory.

Unless she was pregnant.

The elevator doors opened with a ding.

"After you," Kassius said, holding the door.

As she walked down the hall toward the comtesse's suite, she heard his cell phone ring, and his footsteps slowed behind her. She kept walking.

Could she be pregnant?

What if she was?

Her lips curved softly at the idea of having a baby of her own to love, to hold in her arms…a child with Kassius's dark eyes…

No. She couldn't let herself think that way. She was unlikely to be pregnant, and that was a good thing. It would be a disaster right now. A baby was a serious responsibility, and she had nothing to offer. She didn't have money, a proper career, a husband. She didn't even have a real relationship with the baby's father.

All she really knew about Kassius Black was that he was a dangerously sexy billionaire who, for one magical night, had turned her from a servant into a fairy-tale princess in a golden gown. Remembering the way he'd made her feel last night, when she'd nearly wept with ecstasy in his arms, she couldn't even regret losing her chance at ten million dollars. Because in an important way, he'd changed her life.

By seducing her, he'd proven she was desirable, and could feel desire. He'd opened her eyes.

For years, she'd felt invisible, unworthy of love. Now she'd never think of herself as a frigid little virgin again.

But would she soon be a single mother?

Laney could still hear the husky echo of his voice: *I am tired of the bachelor life. I want a family. I want a wife.*

But whatever fantasy he'd been indulging in last night, he'd obviously come to his senses this morning. *It's better to end this quickly.* When Kassius actually took a bride, she would be a beautiful, elegant, sophisticated woman of his own class. A woman like Mimi du Plessis.

Opening the door of the suite, Laney took a deep breath, bracing herself, and walked inside.

Her boss rose from the dining table with a tranquil smile. She murmured, "Have a good time last night?"

Was that a trick question? Was there a chance she wasn't about to be sacked? "Um, yes?"

Then Laney looked across the elegant suite, with all its feminine decor of Louis XVI furniture and wall-to-wall white shag carpeting, and saw her suitcases and a big box of her things sitting on the floor. And she knew she wasn't going to get lucky here.

Desperately, she said, "Madame, please forgive me. I owe you an apology—"

"Too late for that." Coming forward, the comtesse shoved a fifty-euro bill into Laney's hands. "Here."

"What's this?" she said, confused.

"Your last paycheck."

"But my next paycheck is due tomorrow, for two

full weeks. And then there's also eight weeks of paid vacation time you always postponed—"

"Too bad. That's all you get."

"That's illegal!"

"Who's going to fight me? You?" Mimi's expression was hard. "You think you're my equal now, just because Kassius Black took you to bed? You're nothing, Laney. No one. Common street trash." She tossed her blond hair. "Now he's used you, he'll toss you out like garbage—"

"Ah. Mimi. So nice to see you this morning."

Kassius's husky voice made Mimi whirl around with a gasp. "Oh! I didn't expect—"

"Happy New Year." Tucking his phone back into his pocket, he gave her a smile. "I came to help Laney get her things. But also to talk to you."

"To me?" Mimi said.

His dark eyes were warm. "We have a few things to discuss."

Laney felt a stab of wild jealousy that made her sick inside, and no amount of reason could argue her out of it.

"Sir?"

A large man had suddenly appeared in the doorway behind Kassius.

"Ah. Benito." Kassius looked at Laney. "Are those your suitcases?" She nodded. "Is that everything?"

"Of course it's everything," Mimi snapped. "Do you think I want her trash left behind?"

He gave her a hard smile, then turned back to the man. "Please take Miss Henry's suitcases up to the penthouse."

"*Tout de suite*, monsieur."

"Thank you." He looked pointedly at Laney. "Can you manage the box?"

"Of course I can, but I don't see why—"

"I'll see you upstairs later," he interrupted.

She scowled. She didn't understand why he'd apparently asked his bodyguard to take her suitcases up to his penthouse. But she'd clearly been dismissed. And so coldly. Kassius couldn't wait to be alone with Mimi—probably to whisper sweet nothings in her ear and make a date for tonight. While Laney felt exactly like the harlot her ex-boss had implied—standing here like a fool in his oversize robe!

"Sure," Laney said coldly. "Later."

As Benito got her suitcases, she tightened the belt of the robe and lifted up the box that held old books, a plant and her grandmother's quilt. Turning, she left Mimi's suite with as much dignity as she could muster, without looking back.

Once in the hall, she turned to the bodyguard, or whoever he was. "I'll take those suitcases. There's no reason for you to take them upstairs. I'm just going to the airport."

The man shook his head. "Sorry, mademoiselle. Monsieur Black said to take you and the baggage upstairs, so upstairs you will go."

He insisted on taking her up in the elevator to the penthouse—her and the rest of the baggage. Once there, Laney stomped to the bedroom, fuming.

"I'm not going to wait for him!" she yelled back grumpily, but the man had already left. Fine. She'd just change her clothes and leave.

She dug through her suitcases for comfy cotton panties and a bra and started to reach for a white shirt and khaki pants. She stopped, remembering she wasn't anyone's employee. Not anymore.

Instead, she grabbed a brightly colored vintage T-shirt she'd bought at a flea market, advertising a rock concert in Paris in 1976. She put on red jeans that fit her like a glove, skimming tightly over her small waist, curvy hips and butt. Finally, she zipped up a fuzzy purple hoodie and pulled her hair back in a tight, French ponytail, tumbling straight down her back. Then she reached far into her suitcase for a tube of shocking red lipstick. There. Looking at herself in the bedroom's mirror, she smacked her lips with satisfaction.

She was done being anyone's servant.

She was now a woman with prospects.

On second thought, maybe her prospects weren't so great. But she was at least a woman of ambition.

Let's face it—she'd always known that working for the spoiled Mimi du Plessis was not exactly a lifetime occupation. It was time she figured out what she really wanted to do with her life, rather than squandering it by fits and starts.

There were other ways to make money. She could go to community college and train for something useful, like nursing or teaching. At twenty-five years old, she was no longer a kid. She could, and should, start acting like it. She would find a way to have a decent career that didn't leave her depressed and ashamed, one that would let her be close to her family and home. It wouldn't be easy. She'd likely have to work full-time while she attended night classes. But the sacrifice would be worth it.

She missed her family. Her home. Right now she

would have killed for her grandmother's famous jambalaya with dirty rice, or her fried chicken and collard greens. Cheesy fried grits. A little crawfish étouffée or a muffuletta sandwich. She licked her lips at the thought of the tangy olive salad. Or the perfect breakfast—chicory coffee and hot buttery beignets, laced with powdered sugar, from the Café du Monde.

It was time to face the real world, of work and bills, but also, she thought hopefully, of chicory coffee and fried chicken. The real world, with both its hardships and joys.

But she'd always remember the New Year's Eve ball and the night she'd been Cinderella.

Her eyes fell on the exquisite golden ball gown on the floor. Slowly, she picked it up and folded it neatly across the back of a chair. Her fingers traced the sparkles of gold over the netting and tulle.

She would never forget the night. Or the man. Ever.

For the next ten years, when she was working two jobs to pay her way through school and studying all night and eating ramen noodles and beans, she'd remember the one night she'd gone to a ball in Monte Carlo, like Grace Kelly.

Laney stuffed her grandmother's quilt into one of the suitcases and the empty box in the trash. She looked regretfully at the potted geranium. She'd have to leave that behind. She started digging in her small tattered handbag for her phone to order a ride to the airport, then stopped. She had no phone. It had been crushed by Kassius's car.

But it could have been so much worse. After giving him her virginity, after feeling such unbelievable pleasure and sleeping in the protective comfort of his arms all night, she felt how easily she could have fallen for him. A few more such nights, and he could have really broken her heart.

A phone? That could be replaced.

Snapping the suitcase shut, she stood, and looked around one last time at his lavish penthouse suite, with its expensive modern furniture and floor-to-ceiling views. The sun was shining across the bright blue sea.

With a deep breath, she squared her shoulders and turned away. Dragging the two suitcases, she started for the door. Then stopped when it opened and Kassius came in. He looked at the suitcases, and his expression turned dark.

"What do you think you're doing?" he growled.

"What does it look like?" She returned his gaze steadily. "Leaving."

"Leaving?" He gave a low laugh, then closed the door behind him. "Laney, we're just getting started."

She swallowed and hated how her heart fluttered. The expansive suite suddenly felt small with him stretching the walls inside it. All she could see was him. "I assumed when you wanted to be alone with Mimi…"

"That meeting was not personal." His dark eyes glittered. "Just business."

She blinked. "You're offering another loan to her boss? I've met Boris Kuznetsov, by the way. He's nice. Takes good care of his employees. Is that why you keep offering him loans?" she said curiously. "Just to help him out?"

"Something like that." His eyes were hard and veiled as he came closer, holding out a wad of bills. "Here."

Oh, dear heaven, he surely wasn't trying to pay her for what they did in bed last night? She said coldly, "What's that?"

"The money Mimi owes you. Two weeks' salary. Plus all the vacation she owed you for the past two years."

"How did you get it from her?"

The edges of his cruel, sensual lips lifted. "I asked nicely."

Hmm. Truly he had magical powers. She started to reach for the pile of euros, then stopped suspiciously. "What do you want from me in exchange?"

"You think I am trying to buy you?" He sounded amused. "I cannot buy what I already own."

"What are you talking about? You don't own me."

"We made a deal last night." He ran his hand lightly along her shoulder, over her thin vintage T-shirt. "Or did you forget?"

She had sudden memory of his words, huskily spoken in the dark. *If I make you explode with joy, you will surrender everything. You will allow me to take possession of your body and fill you with my child. You will be mine—forever.* She blushed.

"But that was ridiculous. A joke," she stammered. "Verbal foreplay. You don't actually expect me to—"

"I never joke about deals. Or go back on my word." He looked at her in the slanted light of morning. "Are you saying you do?"

The morning light of the Mediterranean caressed the hard edge of his cheekbones, with that lightly etched scar, the dark bristle of his sharp jawline, the boyishly mussed-up dark hair that looked so soft that even now, she longed to run her hands through it again. She forced her hands to remain still and lifted her chin. "In my experience, the wealthy have many whims that quickly change."

"It's not a whim. My proposal was straightforward. I want a family. I want a wife I can trust. You seemed to indicate you might be such a woman, but your only fear was that you would be inadequate in bed. That fear was proven false." He leaned forward. "You surrendered yourself to me, Laney," he whispered, his lips inches from hers. "Everything."

Her mouth went dry. "What kind of choice did you give me? I had no experience. No chance to resist your expert seduction."

Towering over her, he narrowed his eyes. "Are you saying I took you against your will?"

"Of course not," she said helplessly. She spread her hands. "It's just…women are interchangeable for you. An amusement. You switch them out like dirty socks, never committing to any of them."

"I'm willing to commit to you."

She swallowed, shivering with desire. "But it was just fantasy," she said helplessly. "Don't men always say things they don't mean to get women into bed?"

"You feel like home to me." Reaching down, he cupped her cheek. "I intend to marry you, Laney. Soon. Even now, you might be carrying my child."

The idea of marrying Kassius…of having his baby…it was a dream, a silly romantic dream. It couldn't be real! Girls like her didn't marry billionaires!

"You're just toying with me," she whispered.

For an answer, he pulled her into his arms, and kissed her.

His lips were rough and sweet, and as he kissed her, slowly and tantalizingly, her fears and doubts disappeared. She felt lost in the hungry demand of his embrace, the warmth and power of his body against hers. She clung to him, reaching on tiptoe to wrap her arms around his neck, kissing him back with all the long-dormant passion inside her.

He drew away. "You are mine now," he whispered against her lips. "Accept what your body already knows."

She was shaking all over. "Why choose me? We barely know each other!"

"For the same reason I sometimes buy land the moment I see it. Sometimes it's not about the data or growth numbers or years of study." Looking down at her, he stroked her long dark hair. "Sometimes you see something, and you just know."

Was it truly possible? Laney thought of her own parents, who'd known each other their whole childhoods, growing up on the same street, dating all through high school. And look how that turned out.

Was marrying someone you'd known your whole life any less risky than taking a chance on love at first sight?

Love?

Could she love him?

Was she half in love with him already?

She shivered. Infatuation, she told herself. But how would she even know the difference? Maybe love was nothing more than infatuation that lasted.

"But I am going back home to New Orleans," she said numbly. "To get a job."

"No." Kassius ran his hand slowly down her back.

"You're going to stay here and marry me, Laney. You know it. I know it."

She stared up at him, her whole body shaking, feeling wildly alive, her heart in her throat. Oh, this was insane.

"But strangers don't just decide to marry," she breathed.

"Don't they?" Lifting her hand to his lips, he kissed it. She felt the warmth of his breath, the gentle seduction of his lips. She thought how wonderful it was to have someone beside her. Someone watching over her.

"Would it help if I got down on one knee?" His lips curved humorously as he did just that. Pressing his hand to his heart, he said a little mockingly, "Elaine May Henry, will you do me the honor, the incredible glory, of becoming my—"

"Stop, stop!" she cried, her cheeks burning as she pulled him to his feet. "Don't tease!"

He looked down at her, his dark eyes serious.

"You are the one doing the teasing, Laney," he said. "For once and all, what is your answer?"

Her answer?

No.

No, of course.

Except...

Except it was yes.

After a lifetime of being sensible and good, of working all hours and being invisible, she felt the pull of being reckless. Of feeling *alive*. She yearned to be brave enough to do it—to love him—to jump headlong into the unknown. Right or wrong. She wanted to *live*.

She exhaled. "All right."

"You will?"

"Yes."

"There will be no going back," he warned.

"I won't go back." She offered him a trembling smile. "As you said. The deal was made. I honor my promises."

"And I honor mine." Pulling her tight into his arms, he tilted up her chin gently. "From now on, I'll always take care of you, Laney, and everyone you love. You'll never have to worry about anything, now you have my ring on your finger..."

She looked down at her bare left hand.

"Which ring is that?" she teased. She looked around the lavish penthouse suite. "Maybe we can find a ribbon or string or something that we can tie around my finger. A plastic ring from a Cracker Jack box?"

Smiling, he started to pull her toward the door. "I can do better than that."

"Where are we going?"

"The jeweler's."

"I was joking," she protested, then shook her head. "Besides, it's New Year's Day. Won't all the shops be closed?"

His smile widened. "They'll open for me."

CHAPTER FIVE

MONEY, KASSIUS OFTEN reflected, was magic.

He'd built his business empire from nothing, fueled not by any desire for luxury, but his need for power. From the age of sixteen, he'd been grimly determined to make sure he'd never be desperate and helpless again. Never be ignored or left behind. He'd known he'd someday be so powerful and rich that he could get his revenge on the man who'd left him and his beloved mother behind, like garbage.

At eleven, Kassius's relatively happy childhood had ended when his father had abruptly stopped visiting or even sending money. No father. No money. No power. No name. News rushed through their neighborhood that Kassius's parents had never even been married, and just like that, the comfort of their little apartment in a quiet Istanbul street had ended.

He and his mother had suddenly found themselves outcasts. The wives of their neighborhood, distrustful of Emmaline's beauty, immediately froze her out, while their menfolk suddenly believed she would welcome their advances. Kids who'd once been Kassius's friends turned on him at school, repeating cruel taunts they'd heard from their parents. "Your own father doesn't want you—why don't you just curl up and die?"

But in the end it had been Kassius's fragile mother who had died—first her dreams, then her soul, finally her body. She'd been poisoned by waiting.

"Why don't we just sell the apartment and leave, Mama?" Kassius had asked her, stricken and bewildered. She'd shaken her head.

"We can't leave. Your daddy will be back soon…"

But he'd never come back. His Russian father had loved his company and his fortune and his dreams of a Cap Ferrat villa more than he'd loved them.

So that was what Kassius would take from him.

After his mother's death, when he was still a teenager, he'd sold everything he owned and left Istanbul. He'd borrowed as much money as he could get—some from banks, some from less legal, more dangerous loan sharks—to buy a single run-down tenement in an up-and-coming neighborhood in Athens. He'd rebuilt it himself, brick by brick, risking everything, holding back nothing, sleeping on the floor just four hours a night.

He'd put his foot on the throat of success and forced it to cough up what he wanted.

Over two decades, his small real estate holdings had grown into an international conglomerate. He'd bought up beachfront properties in Croatia, factories in Eastern Europe, spreading to Western Europe, then the Americas, Asia and, most recently, Africa.

In the last few years, as Boris Kuznetsov's oil company had run into trouble, he'd pounced, quietly buying up his loans and distressed assets, vacation homes around the world, his jet, the yacht. Kuznetsov still did not realize whom he'd lost them to, and why. But all the man had left now were the two things he cared about most: control of his flailing company, and the gaudy pink villa on Cap Ferrat, a luxurious enclave thirty minutes outside Monaco.

No, Kassius hadn't built his empire because he wanted luxury. He'd wanted power. He'd wanted revenge.

Occasionally, however, the luxury that could be purchased with unlimited money did bring unexpected pleasures. Such as right now.

"Are you sure?" Standing in front of the designer boutique's three-way mirror, Laney looked anxiously back at her deliciously ample backside in the tight, short red dress.

Sitting on a nearby sofa, holding a flute of expensive champagne brought to him by a salesgirl, Kassius stared at her. "You are exquisite."

And she was. The clingy red dress revealed the shape of her hourglass figure to perfection. Kassius couldn't look away from the glory of her wide hips, tiny waist and—he took a quick, shallow breath—those full breasts—

Frowning, Laney turned back to look at herself in the mirror, her lovely heart-shaped face uncertain, her long dark hair tumbling down her shoulders. She bit her full pink lip. "My grandmother would chew me out if she ever saw me walk out of the house in this." Her cheeks turned pink as she looked at the short hem. "I'm embarrassed just to let *you* see me in it!"

Kassius set down the barely tasted champagne. Rising to his feet, he walked a half circle around her. And he smiled.

Money was magic. It had made this all possible.

Designer boutiques and salons had opened just for them, eager for the patronage of the ultrawealthy, mysterious Kassius Black.

Laney had been reluctant to let him buy her anything. So he'd persuaded her with military precision, using logic. First, he'd bought her a replacement phone. That had been relatively easy, because after all, he owed her one. But he'd replaced her old, cheap phone with a top-of-the-line smartphone at ten times the price.

Next, he'd taken her to the most famously exclusive jeweler in Monaco to buy her an engagement ring. As she'd browsed the plain gold bands, he'd quietly purchased in her size a twenty-carat diamond engagement ring set in platinum. He'd overridden her protests that she didn't need anything so expensive. Of course she needed it. She was going to be his bride.

He'd made sure she didn't know how much it cost, however. If she'd known, she would have certainly rebelled at the thought of wearing a sparkling rock on her finger that cost approximately the same as three average houses.

After buying the ring, they'd gone for an elegant lunch near the harbor overlooking the yachts, a slight respite before he'd taken Laney to a salon, where a world-famous hairstylist had left his own New Year's Day house party in Nice to trim and style Laney's dark, lustrous mane. As a manicurist and pedicurist buffed her nails, a makeup artist shaped her brows, adding just the right shade of lipstick, eye shadow and creamy blush.

Laney had never been pampered in quite this way

before. As far as he could tell, she'd never been pampered at all. Obviously. She'd been a virgin who'd—incredibly—believed herself to be frigid until he'd seduced her. She'd been unnoticed by men till now and spent all her time working, providing for her family.

After the salon, she no longer put up a fight. He took her to expensive designer boutiques, buying her clothes, shoes, handbags, an entirely new wardrobe, replacing her thrift store bargains with the chic, sophisticated outfits her new life would require. He'd particularly enjoyed selecting her lingerie. But this—

He lost his breath looking at his bride-to-be.

"Leave us," he said hoarsely.

The two salesgirls and boutique manager hovering in the background glanced at each other uncertainly. Kassius turned to the manager with a cold glare.

"Now."

The manager gave a swift nod and clapped his hands at the two salesgirls, who fled before he followed them out. A second later, they heard the bell of the door as they went out into the cold twilight.

Yes, Kassius thought. Money was magic.

As he turned back smugly to Laney, she was staring at him in disbelief.

"Does everyone always do what you say?"

He came closer to her, his eyes intent. He kissed her bare shoulder, brushing back soft dark tendrils of her hair. "Yes."

He felt her tremble beneath his touch.

"You can't be...thinking that we..." Laney sounded breathless as she looked up at him with big brown eyes. He saw the quick rise and fall of her breasts. But Kassius was past thinking anything.

Pushing her back against the three-way mirror, he roughly kissed her, cupping her magnificent breasts through the tight red dress.

"Not here," she breathed, struggling. "They might walk in…"

"They won't," he whispered huskily, his lips brushing against her ear. "Benito is no doubt entertaining them outside in his lamentable French."

"It's rude kicking them out of their own store, out into the cold after we dragged them here on New Year's Day…"

"They're well paid to wait and not to see or hear anything."

"But if they do—"

"Then let them hear," he said coldly. "Let the whole world hear, and see, and wish you were theirs. Let them be jealous you are mine."

He kissed her roughly, and with a sigh of surrender, she fell back against the mirrored wall. He was rock hard for her, his body straining, as he ran his hands along her hips in the red dress, her bare thighs, the cleavage of her full breasts pressing against the tight fabric.

He needed her. Now.

Roughly, he yanked her short red dress up to her hips, revealing her lace panties.

Kissing her passionately, he lifted her bare legs to wrap around his hips, her back against the mirror. Unzipping his trousers, he roughly yanked her panties aside and without asking permission, he thrust himself inside her with a groan, sheathing himself to the hilt.

She gasped, clinging to him, the tight red dress now pushed up to her waist. Her eyes were closed, her head tossed back with pleasure. She swayed her hips as he pushed inside her, thrusting hard and fast until he heard her cry out, until he felt her shake. Hearing that, feeling it, he exploded inside her.

For a moment, he just held her tight against the wall, her thighs still wrapped around his hips, and she held him. Then, slowly, the world intruded. He released her, and she slid back down to stand in front of him. He zipped up his trousers, smoothed her lace panties and pulled her dress back modestly over her thighs.

"I guess we'll have to buy the dress now." Reaching out, he rubbed smeared lipstick off her chin.

Self-consciously, she touched her skin, then looked up at him accusingly. "Whose fault is that?"

"Yours."

"Mine?"

"For being too desirable." He looked down at her seriously. "I can hardly wait to marry you."

"When did you have in mind?" she said tartly. "You've taken charge of everything today. Are you planning to drag me from here straight to a justice of the peace?" She looked down at the expensive red dress, which hadn't even been paid for yet but was already wrinkled. "Is this my wedding dress?"

He gave a low laugh. "We have dinner reservations at Le Coq d'Or. We can talk about wedding plans over wine."

"Le Coq d'Or?" Her lips parted. "How on earth

did you get reservations there? I heard the comtesse complain about how impossible it is to get in."

He shrugged. "I called them today and gave them my name. They suddenly had space."

"You always get everything you want, don't you?" She sounded grumpy. "You never even have to wait."

"I do sometimes," he said grimly, thinking of the plans for revenge he'd first formulated twenty years before. At her searching glance, he gave her a bland smile. "Shall we tell the boutique staff it's safe to come back?"

Ten minutes later, Benito and their sedan's driver were stacking yet more of their shopping bags into the trunk. Kassius held the car door open for Laney, who was now wearing a long, expensive, belted black coat over her red dress, which he'd insisted she should wear, to keep off the cool air.

"You want to drive?" She looked surprised. "But it's a lovely evening. Le Coq d'Or is just up the hill. Why not walk?"

"*Just up the hill?*" He snorted. "It's a half-hour walk."

"So?"

He looked pointedly at her feet, now shod in wickedly expensive stilettos. "In those?"

Her ankle turned slightly on the sidewalk, proving his point. She regained her balance and glared at him. "So?"

"Most women I know complain if they have to walk more than a hundred meters in shoes like that. And they're more accustomed to wearing them."

Laney tossed her head, looking offended as she retorted, "Most of your other women were probably not accustomed to working sixteen to twenty hours a day on their feet."

What was she trying to prove? He looked at her, amused. "True."

"So." Her chin lifted, and her eyes glittered. "We're walking."

Kassius shrugged. "As you wish." He gave his bodyguard and driver a nod, and they got into the sedan and drove on. Tossing her head, she started walking with a determined stride. Ten steps later, she wobbled in her stiletto heels and had to grab his arm.

"You sure you're up for this?" he inquired.

"It's your fault if I have trouble."

"Because I bought you the shoes?"

"Because you bought me such an obscenely huge engagement ring." She looked down at it. "It weighs five pounds. No wonder my balance is off."

Kassius gave a low laugh. Laney fascinated him. She seemed to be so many women, all at once. At the ball, she'd looked like an enchanted princess from a fairy tale. That morning when he'd proposed to her, she'd looked like a bohemian college student in her vintage rock T-shirt and red jeans—vibrant, chaotic, alive.

Now…in the sleek belted black coat and stilettos… with the red dress beneath…

He shuddered with desire, already wanting her again. He took her hand, looking down at her. "We could skip dinner," he said huskily. "And go back to the penthouse."

She stared up at him. "Seriously?"

"Why not?"

"Are you trying to starve me?"

"Can't have that." He looked appreciatively at her curves and sighed with regret. "All right. Dinner first."

Her triumphant expression lasted only about ten minutes, which was when the road started to go sharply uphill. Soon, she was wincing with every step.

"I'll call my driver."

"Why?" she said through gritted teeth. "Are you tired?"

She was determined, he had to give her that. But he didn't understand why she was being so stubborn about this. "Just kick your shoes off and walk barefoot."

"I'm fine," she panted, forcing her lips into a bright, fake smile. "Six-inch stiletto heels are comfortable to me. Just like fuzzy bunny slippers!"

When they were two blocks away from the restaurant on the Boulevard du Jardin Exotique, she really started to stumble. The edges of her skin, where they were crammed into the shoes, looked red and swollen. The back of her ankle had started to bleed. It was too much. With a low growl, Kassius swept her up into his arms.

"What are you doing?" she demanded.

"I'm not letting you kill yourself for the sake of your pride, you little fool." Ignoring her weak struggles, he carried her the rest of the way down the block to the expensive, exclusive restaurant with vast windows overlooking the Monte Carlo district of Monaco and all of the bay.

"*Bonsoir,*" he said pleasantly to the valets and doorman, who were goggling at them. The staff at Le Coq d'Or had no doubt seen a great deal of peculiar behavior they were paid to overlook from their wealthy, spoiled clientele, but apparently this was a new one, even for them.

"Put me down!" Laney hollered, then proceeded to curse Kassius roundly and colorfully until the other men's eyes widened farther still. She cursed him until he set her down and her feet actually touched the ground, when she visibly winced and her cheeks turned pale with pain.

Now Kassius was the one to curse. Getting down on one knee before her, he yanked off her stiletto heels, one after the other. "Laney, what are you trying to prove?"

"Nothing!"

"These aren't hiking boots, you little fool."

"I know, but—"

"But what?"

Her cheeks burned, and she looked away.

And he suddenly knew.

"You're tougher than any of them, Laney. Better than any woman I've ever been with. Is that what you're trying to prove? Well, you are." He handed the shoes to her. "And for the record, a million times sexier, too."

"I wasn't trying to prove anything." But her pale cheeks turned red, and he knew he'd guessed correctly. She mumbled, "And I am not sexier."

Looking down, he said softly, "Want me to prove how much I want you? Right here and now?"

"You wouldn't," she breathed, her eyes big and incredibly appealing. But by the nervous look in her face, she was remembering their earlier encounter at the designer boutique. And probably wondering if he intended to take savage possession of her body right in front of the restaurant, with the doorman and valets looking on.

"But I can't have you faint from hunger." He gave her a wicked grin. Leaning forward, he whispered, "Not with what I've got planned for later."

Her eyes went big, and she licked her lips, which just made him want to kiss her more.

It was amazing to Kassius how even though he'd just made love to her an hour ago, he already wanted her again. He wondered if his desire for her would ever be sated, and doubted it. But that would just have to wait until they got back to the penthouse. Tucking her stilettos into her expensive new handbag, he led Laney into the expensive restaurant.

The maître d' spotted him, and his expression became obsequious. "Monsieur Black, welcome. We have your table ready." The man's glance fell to Laney's bare feet, and for a moment his mien faltered, but then his smile reasserted itself. "May I take your coats? This way, if you please, monsieur, mademoiselle."

Laney held Kassius's hand tightly as they walked through the crowded restaurant, past the elegant diners and buzz of polyglot conversation in French, German, Russian, Italian, English, Japanese and others. Le Coq d'Or was internationally famous, and well-heeled patrons often flew here on their private jets for a hard-to-get dinner reservation. But conversation seemed to stop as they passed by.

She clung to his hand, and whispered, "They're looking at me."

He glanced back at her indulgently. "Because you're beautiful."

"Because I'm barefoot. They think I'm a hick."

"You are with me. You can be whatever you want to be."

You can be whatever you want to be.

His own words brought him up short. For a moment, Kassius was distracted by a flash of light through the wide windows, of the lowering twilight sun sparkling across the silver sea. A memory floated back to him of his mother's raspy words as she lay dying.

"You can be whatever you want to be, darlin'." He could still hear her low laugh. She'd never lost her lilt, the drawl of the American South. "Believe it or not, my own parents wanted me to stay home and be a political wife in a big mansion."

"So why didn't you?" he'd asked her then in a low voice, heartsick over her illness and nearly overwhelmed by grief and rage at what he'd just discovered about his long-absent father.

"I wanted adventure," Emmaline Cash had whispered. "And I got it." Smiling through her tears, his mother squeezed his arm weakly. "It's the secret of life. You can be whatever you want to be, darlin'. As long as you're willing to pay the price…" Her words ended in fierce coughing. From her bed, she'd motioned around the tiny, sagging apartment on the edges of Istanbul. "You don't have to settle for what others want for you or for the life you're born in. You can decide."

He'd looked down at his mother's tiny, fragile form beneath the blankets, feeling like he'd been kicked between the ribs. She was too young to die. She'd barely lived.

"Do you have any regrets, Mama?" he'd choked out.

She gave him a trembling smile. "I wish I could live long enough to see the man you'll be, the family you'll have someday." Her smile abruptly faded. When she spoke again, her voice was a low rasp he'd never heard before. "And I wish the first time your father came up with excuses why he couldn't marry me I'd let myself see him for the liar he was, rather than make excuses. If I'd only been brave enough to leave him right then and there, our lives could have been so different! Maybe I could have found another man who would have loved us. Cherished us. But I was so sure—" Her dark eyes shone with sudden anguish as she put her hand over his. "If someone ever shows you the truth of who they are, if they lie or cheat or betray you, promise me you'll believe them the first time!" Her voice broke on a sob. "Don't destroy your life, or your child's, wishing and hoping and pretending they'll change—"

"Kassius?" Laney said.

He abruptly focused on her, coming back to the present as they were seated at a prime table by the windows. Numbly, he helped her with her chair then took his own seat as the waiter handed them menus and poured their water.

She looked at him thoughtfully. "So I can be anything I want to be, huh? How about prima ballerina, or a circus lion tamer?"

Kassius gave a small smile. "Why not?"

He wondered what she would say if he told her about his past, told her what had driven him to become the man he was today. She was dying to know. She, like every woman. Like every business com-

petitor or shareholder. They all claimed they needed
to know the particulars of his past, as if that could
be beneficial, as if that would inspire trust and co-
operation.

The truth was, if they knew what had driven him
since he was sixteen years old, if they knew his real
name, they would only find a way to use that information against him. They would use his old grief as
a wedge in his soul to devour him, to destroy him.

Reveal weakness to no one. It had been a hard lesson to learn, when his first business partner, someone he'd trusted, had run off with his money, setting
Kassius back an entire year of backbreaking work.
Showing your throat even to the meekest sheep would
only reveal weakness and give the sheep the sharp
greedy teeth of a wolf. He wouldn't give anyone the
opportunity to go for his jugular.

But the most important lesson in success was from
the example of his own father. He'd learned to be
selfish and pursue his own desires. No matter how
it might hurt others. He'd learned to only care about
himself.

He'd chosen Laney not just because of her deep
sexual appeal, but also her sweetness, her innocence.
Her kind heart. He'd thought perhaps he could let
himself be vulnerable with her, after they were wed.

But now he suddenly realized he couldn't take that
risk. If even Laney knew his weaknesses, she could
use it against him. She could leave him, or betray him.

He would never give her that power. She would get
no ammunition from him—no bullets from his past
she could use against him.

"L think you'd make an excellent lion tamer,"

he said mildly and opened the menu. "What looks good?"

She looked at her own menu, filled with very elegant and precious delicacies such as foamy quail eggs, and sighed. "What I wouldn't give for some good Southern cooking right now." She brightened. "Maybe we could stop at the supermarket on the way back to your penthouse."

"Southern?" He looked up sharply. "You know how to cook Southern cuisine?"

"Sure," she said with a shrug. "Fried chicken, grits, collard greens. Gumbo, dirty rice, muffuletta sandwiches. All that stuff. My grandma taught me."

The waiter came to take their order. By this time Kassius's mind was so full of Louisiana cooking that he barely cared about some impossibly exclusive three-star French restaurant. He impatiently ordered them both the tasting menu and a fine red Bordeaux, a 2005 Château Lafite Rothschild. As the waiter departed with a bow, Kassius leaned forward. "I've been trying to hire a Louisiana chef for my ski chalet in Gstaad, but it's hopeless."

"You must not be looking in the right places." Laney smiled at a different waiter, who brought a bread bowl to their table. She immediately helped herself to a piece of the plump, fresh bread and slathered it with butter. "Where I'm from, everyone knows how to cook."

"Didn't you once work as assistant to that world-famous Louisiana chef?"

She frowned. "How did you know that?"

Oh. Right. She didn't know about the investigator.

Shrugging, he gave her a charming smile. "I heard it somewhere."

"Huh." She looked a little confused, then continued, "Sure, I learned some stuff from him. But if you ask me, my grandmother is the best cook in New Orleans."

"That's quite a statement."

"It's true, and she taught me everything she knows."

A shiver went through Kassius. Sitting at this exclusive restaurant on the Côte d'Azur for a meal that might easily cost fifteen hundred euros a plate, his mouth was suddenly watering for something more simple. The home cooking of long ago. When he'd had a home. And when someone had cooked for him, not for money, but for love.

The waiter brought the wine and poured a bit in a large wineglass. Kassius swirled it, sipped, then nodded. The waiter poured for them both.

"I haven't been home for over two years. I miss it."

"What do you miss?" he asked curiously.

"My family. The city. The food. The smell of cypress and magnolias. Everything." She sighed as she sipped her wine and settled back in her chair. "Even Mardi Gras. What a party. The whole city goes crazy." Crossing her leg, she bounced her bare leg. Her toenails were a wicked, glossy red. He had a hard time not staring at her crossed leg, bouncing. She continued dreamily, "Nothing but parades and music and food, and the whole city out of their mind with joy."

"Sounds...nice." His mother used to speak wistfully about Mardi Gras, too. But he'd never been to New Orleans, not once, or seen the house where she'd been born on St. Charles Avenue. Her wealthy, disapproving parents had disinherited her at nineteen, when Emmaline had run off to be a stewardess rather than accepting the decorous marriage they'd arranged for her. Sixteen years later, after Emmaline had been abandoned by the father of her son, when she was desperate and grievously sick, she'd humbled her pride and written her parents to ask for their help. She'd asked them to promise to take her teenage son, whom they'd never met, if she died from her illness.

Their answer had been scathing.

You made your bed, Emmaline, they'd told her. *Now lie in it.*

His mother had never told Kassius about this, of course. But after her death, he'd found the letter from her parents, Eugene and Thelma Cash, tucked next to his own birth certificate.

Kassius's grandparents wrote him after her death, to try to take back their cruel words, to make him part of their lives. "We thought she just wanted money. We didn't realize she was actually dying." He threw their letter in the trash and left for Athens.

Later, after he'd made his fortune, after his grandparents had both died, he'd bought their old house in New Orleans. He'd had it destroyed. He'd never wanted to see it.

But suddenly, Kassius wanted to see New Orleans through Laney's eyes.

"Sounds like a good place for a honeymoon."

At this, she abruptly stopped bouncing her leg. "What are you saying?"

"We could even get married there. Isn't Mardi Gras next month?"

She stared at him, her eyes joyful. "You mean it? My family could be there?"

She seemed far more thrilled by the prospect of having a party with her family than she'd been by the over half a million euros he'd spent on her today. He found he liked being the object of her gratitude, the person who gave her joy. He liked it very much. He wanted more of it.

"Sure, if that's what you want. By the way—" he took a sip of the red wine "—since you were so concerned about your family's financial situation, I have instructed my business manager to call them and make sure they have any money they need, without limit or question."

Her brown eyes were huge. "Seriously?"

"Of course."

"Oh, Kassius—" Then she bit her lip as her expression faded. "But they can be proud, especially my father. I'm not sure they will accept money from you."

"Of course they will," he said firmly. "It is my responsibility now to provide for all of you. And money doesn't matter. It's not what I care about."

"What do you care about?"

He looked at her.

"Finishing this damn dinner," he said frankly, "so I can take you to bed."

"Oh, just you wait." Ignoring all the high-powered tycoons and socialites at surrounding tables, Laney rose from her chair. Her beautiful face was suffused with joy as she went to him and climbed in his lap. He could feel the entire restaurant goggling at the sight of Laney in the red dress as, wrapping her arms around him, she bent her head and whispered in his ear, "I intend to thank you tonight. Very thoroughly."

Kassius felt fire whip through his blood, from his brain to his groin. And though they hadn't even been served their dinner yet, it was all he could do not to immediately raise his hand and call for the check.

"Oh, no," Laney whispered aloud. She stared down at the bathroom scale, which was giving her news she didn't like at all. She looked at herself in the mirror. Her face was green.

But was it any wonder she felt so ill and run-down? For the last eight weeks, since they'd left Monaco, she'd had too much of everything.

Too much travel, for a start. Too many days with Kassius on his private jet, accompanying him on business trips around the world, from London to Berlin to Tokyo to Johannesburg to Sydney to Nairobi to Santiago and back to their home base in London. She felt exhausted just thinking about it.

Too much shopping. In each new city, Kassius had insisted on showering her with expensive gifts of clothes, handbags, shoes and jewelry, when she already had so much, her big walk-in closet at the town house in London was threatening to explode. She hadn't yet had time to wear half of what he'd bought her.

Too much time spent planning their upcoming wedding in New Orleans. Laney would have been fine with a simple ceremony she planned herself, with a few friends and maybe some rum punch and her grandmother's homemade Cajun dinner, but Kassius had insisted she hire a wedding planner in New Orleans to manage everything. Which meant Laney was constantly on the phone with her, and spending far too many hours over ridiculous decisions, like what candy color the iPads in the guest gift bags should be.

And worst of all—Laney had suffered through far too many of Kassius's business dinners in expensive restaurants, where the red-faced, oversize men all seemed to have stomachs of iron, and ate huge dinners of steak, foie gras and baked potatoes covered in butter and sour cream, then smoked cigars as they washed it all down with scotch and drank oceans of expensive wine. Their girlfriends and wives, skeletal as fashion decreed, seemed to meekly subsist on lettuce leaves and an occasional gin and diet tonic.

Kassius thought that was ludicrous and had threatened to end their engagement if Laney ever followed their example. "I like every single pound of you," he'd told her firmly. "Don't lose a single one."

Laney had liked it when Kassius said it, but now she was in a panic. Because just this last week, without trying, she'd lost five pounds.

All the fault of this exhausting lifestyle, she thought grumpily. And since they had sex at all hours, she hadn't had nearly enough sleep. No wonder her body was breaking down. She'd felt so nauseated that four days ago, she'd actually sent Kassius off alone on his business trip to Hong Kong. He'd been none too pleased about it.

She hadn't been, either. She hated having him so far away from her, even just for a few days. Though she didn't always love the forced luxury of their over-scheduled, shallow lifestyle, she did love living with Kassius, being in his arms, in his bed. She loved that he was the first person she saw in the morning, and the last person she saw at night. It was starting to feel like…a relationship.

She shivered at the thought.

All the plans she'd once had for her life seemed like pale shadows compared to her daily joy of being with him. All thoughts of going to college or getting a job had flown out the window. The thought horrified her. Here she was, a twenty-first-century woman, but all she wanted to do, all she wanted to be, was the lover—the *wife*—of this intoxicating, infuriating, sexually electrifying man.

And soon, the mother of his child? They were going to be a family. As someone who'd always had to work for a paycheck, just being able to spend her days with him, *for* him, made her deliriously happy. Even if the activities that filled their days weren't ones she would have necessarily chosen, somehow having Kassius beside her made it endurable. Even magical. Suddenly, all the fairy tales were making sense.

Did Kassius feel the same? she wondered. He hadn't liked leaving her in London. He wanted her with him constantly. It was the reason why, after eight weeks together, he still hadn't let her visit her family in New Orleans.

"You'll see them soon enough, at the wedding," he'd growled. "Until then, I need you with me. You're my woman."

Words that made her toes curl in happiness.

He was due to return from Hong Kong tonight. But it worried her. After four days spent alone in Kassius's huge London town house, barely getting out of bed, she'd thought she'd be feeling better by now. She'd thought she would be back to her old self, and able to welcome him home properly—and by properly, she meant in bed.

Since they'd left Monaco, London had been their new home base. She'd liked the city from the moment they'd arrived at a private airport and a car had arrived to whisk them to a fancy neighborhood that Kassius told her was called Knightsbridge.

At the four-story town house, Laney had met additional house staff, besides the bodyguards and driver carrying their luggage. Four people were waiting to formally greet them as they walked in.

"Welcome home, sir," a thin, elderly woman said.

"Thank you, Mrs. Beresford. I'd like you to meet my fiancée, Miss Laney Henry."

Mrs. Beresford had shaken her hand politely.

But later, as Kassius led Laney up the sweeping stairs of the elegant mansion, she whispered to him, "I don't think your housekeeper likes me."

He'd looked at her, surprised, then shook his head in amusement. "She's just nervous."

That thought surprised Laney so much she stopped on the stairs. "Her, nervous?"

"You're her new boss."

"Me?"

He smiled. "As my wife, you'll rule the home, and I have five of them—houses, I mean—with a paid staff at each. You're now their boss."

The thought astonished Laney. Her, the boss?

"Really?" she squeaked.

"Why? Are you afraid?"

Terrified. "Um…and they all live here?"

"Only Mrs. Beresford. But they all exist to serve our desires." His eyes darkened, turned hungry. "As you, Laney, exist to serve mine."

Then he'd taken her to bed.

But Laney's whole life hadn't been spent in bed, unfortunately. Or even on his very comfortable private jet, zipping to exotic locales.

Sadly, she was also expected to be his hostess, and his companion at social events and those awful business dinners. Those were the worst. She always feared she wasn't interesting enough and they were laughing behind her back. When it all got too stressful, the only good cure was calling her family for a nice long chat. But even those weren't the same as they used to be.

When she'd first phoned her grandmother and father to tell them she was engaged to Kassius, they hadn't exactly been overjoyed. Her grandmother had been shocked and dubious. Her father had been downright mad.

And now, eight weeks later, not much had changed. Each time she called them, it was the same.

"You sure about this wedding, Laney May?" her grandmother kept repeating. "You just met the man, and marriage lasts a long time. It ain't just about great sex."

"Gran!" she cried, embarrassed. But talking to her father was even worse.

"What kind of man is he, to propose marriage after two days' acquaintance?" her father growled into the phone.

"We just met, and we knew…" She blushed. "Kassius is amazing, Dad."

"So amazing he won't let you come home for a visit? So amazing he can't be bothered to come meet your family and ask your father for your hand in marriage?"

"Of course he's dying to meet you and Gran. He's just such an important man, Dad, and so very busy…"

It had sounded pretty lame, even to her own ears.

"Busy?" he'd said scornfully. "Doing what—counting his money? Flying you all over the world on that private jet of his, traveling everywhere *but* your home? Face it, Laney May. The man doesn't respect you. And he sure doesn't respect us."

No, talking to her family wasn't nearly as comforting as it used to be. But at least she had assurances from Kassius's business manager that her family had been informed they now had access to any and all financial resources they might desire. She'd been a little surprised they'd consider his offer, given their opinions about him, but since they hadn't said no, she tried to take it as a good sign.

Her wedding day was almost here. She and Kassius were supposed to leave for New Orleans tomorrow, and their wedding would be held the day after. It was a tight schedule, but he'd been busy wrapping up a deal in Asia.

At least her wedding dress was finished—her grandmother had sent Laney her wedding gown, used fifty years earlier when she'd begun her own long, happy marriage to her grandfather. The elegant 1960s gown had been recut and tailored to Laney's size, and lengthened for her extra two inches of height. Last week, when she'd first seen herself in it, she'd cried.

"Everything is set. Your wedding will be perfect, Miss Henry," the wedding planner had told her that morning over the phone.

But it wouldn't be such a perfect wedding, Laney thought unhappily now, if she was violently ill into her wedding flowers.

Maybe she should call a doctor. Because she was really starting to worry. In the four days since Kassius left, she'd existed on saltine crackers and lemon-lime soda. It seemed strange she wasn't feeling better. She felt so tired all the time. And her breasts still felt so sensitive, when Kassius hadn't made love to her for days. It was almost as if...

She sucked in her breath.

"Is there anything else you require, madam?" Mrs. Beresford peeked in at the door of the front sitting room. "I'm going to retire for the night." She frowned, coming closer. "Are you quite all right, Miss Henry?"

Laney sat up straight on the sofa. "Can you help me find a doctor who does house calls?"

Two hours later, after Dr. Khan congratulated her and left the house, Laney walked back to the sofa in a daze.

She wasn't sick. She hadn't been feeling ill because she'd eaten too many fattening meals or traveled too much or had too much sex...or actually—she blushed—her situation was the result of precisely that last one.

She was pregnant.

"Oh, my dear," Mrs. Beresford said gently, patting her on the shoulder, "I'm so happy for you. I did wonder all week if that might be the cause..."

"You did?" Of course Mrs. Beresford knew.

Household servants were always the first to know. Often even before their employers did.

After the kindly older woman left for her own suite, Laney hunkered down on the sofa to wait for Kassius to come home from the airport. She cuddled beneath her grandmother's homemade quilt, feeling dazed as she put her hands over her belly.

A baby. She'd soon be holding a sweet baby in her arms. Kassius's and hers.

She felt overwhelmed by emotion, caught between joy and anxiety. Her family's words came back to haunt her.

Face it, Laney May. The man doesn't respect you.

But Kassius did respect her. She knew he did. He always told her she was beautiful and how much he desired her. He told her he couldn't wait to marry her and start a family. He thanked her for accompanying him to business dinners—"You're a natural, you charm everyone"—and as for her cooking skills— well, his enthusiasm for that knew no bounds.

On Valentine's Day, she'd made him a romantic dinner in the house's enormous kitchen, with all of his favorite dishes.

"I'm in love," Kassius had moaned, his expression one of pure ecstasy. Unfortunately, he was looking at the fried chicken as he said it.

And maybe that was the problem.

Laney shivered under her grandma's quilt.

She didn't just want him to love her fried chicken, or her jambalaya, or her gumbo. She wanted him to love *her*.

Because she was in love with him.

She couldn't deny it anymore. Couldn't tell herself

it was just a crush. Honestly, she'd been in love with him from the day he'd hit her with his car.

For her, it had been love at first sight.

But for him...?

Kassius never mentioned love. And though she tried to convince herself that he, too, must have also loved her at first sight—otherwise, why would he have proposed marriage?—she feared she was deluding herself. He had such hard edges. He rarely spoke of his feelings, or desires beyond sex or food or the next business deal. He sometimes spent hours working out at the gym, coming back bruised from sparring at the dojo. What drove him so hard?

She wished she knew. But when she asked him personal questions, he changed the subject. He didn't ask her about her feelings or her past, either.

If only he would trust her enough to let her in. If only he could love her. If only the news of their coming baby could be the crack that would let light, and love, into his heart!

The bodyguard peeked in an hour later.

"I just heard Mr. Black's plane isn't expected till later. Do you need anything, Miss Laney?"

She smiled up at him from the sofa, grabbing a magazine. Winter twilight was starting to fade through the windows, but she felt too exhausted to bother turning on a light. "No, thank you, Benito. I'm good."

And he, too, departed for his own suite of rooms in the basement, where he was always available in case of trouble, as a backup to the security alarm in their very safe neighborhood.

Laney's eyes soon grew heavy. She must have

fallen asleep, because she woke in darkness when she heard the front door slam. Hearing Kassius's voice, she sat up on the sofa, ready to call out his name.

Then she heard a woman's low, throaty laugh in the foyer. "You're taking a risk, bringing me here."

Heart pounding, Laney sank down lower on the sofa, lifting the quilt back up to her forehead so they wouldn't see her as they walked by the open doorway.

"What will you do if your sweet little Laney finds out?" The woman continued. Her voice was familiar. Very familiar.

"She won't. She's a deep sleeper, especially lately." Kassius's voice was low and cool. "Better to do it here, where no one can see us."

"Ah, so the little angel sleeping peacefully upstairs has no idea what you're up to? I thought you two were so close. I heard you were engaged."

"We are."

"Funny sort of engagement. Seems she went from being my servant to yours."

Hardly breathing, Laney peeked over the back of the sofa to see Kassius, looking devastatingly handsome as ever in his suit covered by a long black coat. And the woman with him—her old boss, Mimi du Plessis!

"Here," Kassius said to her, grabbing a black velvet box from a drawer. "As promised."

She opened it and smiled. "You're a man of your word." Lifting her blond hair off her neck, she glanced back at him flirtatiously. "Put it on me."

Setting down the box on the entryway table, he lifted out an exquisite diamond necklace and wrapped it around her throat. "There. Good?"

"Good." Turning back, she looked up at him and observed, "You know, it might have been cheaper for you to just marry me instead of paying me in gifts."

"Or not."

"Or not," she agreed. She gave him a mock salute. "Until next time."

Mimi du Plessis walked out of the foyer, her sharp little heels clacking against the marble floor. When the front door closed behind her, Kassius exhaled, pulling off his long black coat. His shoulders looked weary.

Trembling, Laney rose from the sofa and rushed into the brightly lit foyer. When Kassius saw her, his tired face lit up. But she was way past caring about that now.

"What the hell is going on?" she demanded.

It was so unlike her to curse, he stared at her in shock. "Laney—"

"What was *she* doing here? Why did you give her jewelry? Why?"

His expression shuttered. Turning back to his laptop bag, he pulled out his computer, then glanced back at the dark sitting room. "Eavesdropping, were you? Waiting in the dark to see what you could discover?"

"I fell asleep on the sofa, waiting to tell you—" She bit off her words. "It doesn't matter! I heard you!"

"And just what do you think you heard?"

"Are you having an affair?" she choked out, feeling wretched.

"Are you serious?"

A wave of nausea hit her, and she was suddenly afraid she might throw up into the potted palm at the bottom of the stairs. "Is she the one you actually love? Is that it? Was that why you proposed to me—just to make her jealous?"

Kassius's jaw clenched. "If you're going to talk crazy, I'm going to bed."

But as he turned away from her, Laney's knees sagged back toward the wall. Suddenly he was there, catching her. He searched her face fiercely.

"What's wrong?"

"I'm fine." Her teeth were chattering. "Just furious, and..." *Terrified.* That's what she was. Terrified.

"You're not fine," he said, and without asking for permission, he lifted her up into his arms.

She felt too weak to fight as he carried her upstairs. Setting her down softly on their bed, he poured her a glass of water from the en suite bathroom. "Why didn't you tell me you were ill?"

"It's—nothing," she said weakly.

He stood by the bed. His lips curved downward. "I'm calling a doctor."

"I already saw one..."

"You did?"

"Just tell me the truth," she pleaded. She grabbed his arm, looking up at him. The nausea was starting to abate, but her heart was filled with pain. "Do you love her?"

He looked down at her in the shadowy bedroom. "Of course I don't."

"Because if you do—"

"I'll never love her. Or anyone."

His answer, far from being reassuring, made everything even worse.

"Anyone?" she said through dry lips. She took a

deep breath, looking up at him with anguish. "You'll never love me?"

He sat down on the bed beside her. "No," he said quietly. "Sorry."

Her face was hot, her eyes burning with shame. "Won't—or can't?"

"What's the difference?"

"Then why did you propose to me?" she said hoarsely.

"For the reasons I told you." Reaching out, he stroked a tendril of her hair. "Sex. Home. A family. Children."

"But all that is supposed to spring from love." She licked her dry lips, tried to be hopeful. "Maybe in time…"

His expression hardened. "No, Laney." He pulled away. "I thought you understood. I'm not a sentimental man. It's not in my nature."

"What happened to you?" she choked out. "To turn you like this?"

Kassius stared at her for a moment. Then, rising from the bed, he went to the window. He pushed it open and took a breath of the cold February air.

Winter in London had a hard chill, different from Monaco or New Orleans. Or maybe it was Laney's soul that felt so suddenly frozen. Maybe it was her heart.

She watched a curl of cold winter wind blow against the curtains as, for a long moment, he looked out blankly at the iced-over city. Then he looked at her. "Love was never part of the deal. You knew that."

"I didn't, I never knew that!" she cried.

He exhaled. "Well, you know now." He looked at her. "Do you want out of our engagement?"

Laney might have said yes, she wanted out. If she had known from the beginning that he would never love her…that he would only give his money and his body but never his soul, not even the tiniest bit.

But it was too late now. She couldn't leave. Not when she was pregnant with his child. After growing up with the heartbreak of having her mother put her own selfish, ultimately futile pursuit of happiness ahead of her family's needs, Laney had sworn she'd never do the same. Nothing mattered more to her than family. Nothing. Her unborn baby deserved a father, especially a loving one, like she believed Kassius would be. And as long as he loved their baby, she told herself she could live without him loving her.

But oh, the thought hurt. She wanted him to love her. She wanted it desperately.

If only she could believe there was some chance, no matter how small…

"If you can't accept what I offer you," Kassius said quietly, "perhaps it would be better if I just let you go."

Biting her lip, she looked up at him. "Perhaps we could just get to know each other better. I know you don't like to talk about yourself," she added hastily, "but I could start by telling you about me. How I grew up, and—"

"I already know everything," he interrupted, sounding bored. "I had a private investigator pull up a dossier. I know absolutely everything about you."

She froze. "You do?"

He nodded.

"About—my father's injury? And how my mother left us?"

"Everything."

"Since when?"

"Since before the New Year's Eve ball."

So before their first kiss, Kassius had already known about her private griefs—her father's injury, her mother's abandonment and death. While she knew almost nothing about him at all.

Laney felt sick. Violated. "If you wanted to know about my past, you could have just asked me."

"More efficient just to buy the information."

A chill went through her. "What made you this way?"

"What way?" he said.

"So cold," she whispered. "Sometimes you're so warm, and other times...so cold. Like you don't care about anyone and you prefer it that way."

"That's about right."

"Yes, it is, isn't it?" She gave a low, strangled laugh. "I should have known, just from your wealth."

"What's that supposed to mean?"

Laney looked at him steadily. "Normal people do not become billionaires. The relentless pursuit of money requires cold sacrifice and single-mindedness that few people have."

His sensual lips curved. "You're just now figuring that out?"

"The only ones who can do it have a hole in their hearts," she whispered. She looked at him in the shadowy bedroom. "What caused the hole in your heart, Kassius, that's made you willing to sacrifice your own happiness in pursuit of money and power?"

He stared at her, his jaw tight. "I was poor and

made myself rich. You think that proves me heart-less?"

"That's not what I said—"

"What do you want from me, Laney?" he de-manded.

"I want you to…" *To let me love you. And I want you to love me.* But she couldn't say those things, be-cause she already knew what his answer would be—dismissive, cold, sarcastic. So licking her lips, she said, "I want to know a little more about you. As your future wife, I surely have that right. The obligation!"

He rolled his eyes. "Fine. What exactly do you want to know?"

"For starters—where are you from?"

"Lots of places." He gave her a cynical smile. "I'm a citizen of the world."

"Sure," she said impatiently. "But where were you born?"

"Why does that matter?"

"Your first language—"

"I speak six of them. They all hold an equal im-portance to me."

"You must have a passport."

"I have a few." She wondered if he was joking, but he bared his teeth in a smile. "All perfectly legal, of course. I make large investments in many countries. You heard about the building project in Malaysia that will be the tallest skyscraper in the world? That's mine. Governments are grateful. I bring high-paying jobs for their citizens."

"And profit for yourself."

"Of course. Why else would I do it?"

She pounced. "So why do you keep lending money

to Boris Kuznetsov? His company is on life support. You have to know you'll never get that money back. Even Mimi said so. In what way is that profitable?"

His expression turned hard. "It's not your concern."

"What does it have to do with Mimi? Why did you bring her here and give her diamonds? If you're not having an affair—"

"You want to know me? You won't learn this way. Talking isn't how people reveal themselves. It's how they hide." His jaw tightened. "I'm not having an affair with Mimi du Plessis, believe me. I'll never betray you, Laney. If you don't want me to lie to you, don't ask me questions I can't answer."

"Can't or won't?"

"I told you. It's the same thing."

"I'm to just stay out of your life—is that it? Just be sweet and grateful and warm your bed, without ever challenging you? Mimi was right." She lifted her chin. "You want a servant. Not a wife."

"I am who I am. If you don't like it, leave."

His voice was cold. As if he didn't care either way. As if he could go out and get himself a new fiancée tomorrow. Which, she thought miserably, he probably could.

While Laney was utterly trapped, both by duty and devotion.

She'd let herself fall in love him, based on the exhilarating way he'd made her feel. She hadn't bothered to ask serious questions or properly know him. She'd just let herself fall for him like a stone.

Laney's fingertips traced the huge diamond on her left hand. She yearned to give in to the demands of her pride, to rip the ring off her finger and throw it back in his face. She yearned to tell him exactly where he could take the ring and his cold heart.

But she couldn't. Not now. She was pregnant with his baby.

Laney thought longingly of her grandmother, and her father, and home, and the smell of magnolia blossoms, the bright red bougainvillea and weeping cypress trees. Her family had been right about everything. Romantic dreams had blinded her to reality.

Feeling heartsick, she whispered, "What about a baby?"

His expression changed. "What about it?"

"If we…had a child. You couldn't love our baby, either?"

"That's different. I'd always protect my children, and make sure they felt secure and loved."

She exhaled, closing her eyes. That decided her.

Her unborn baby hadn't been the one to make such a foolish mistake, getting engaged and pregnant and falling in love with a man before she ever thought to ask if he could someday love her. Laney was the one who'd made the mistake. She'd be the one to suffer for it.

Laney swallowed, feeling dizzy. She forced herself to say, "I have something to tell you."

Kassius looked irritated, as if he assumed she was going to say something he didn't want to deal with. Like *I love you*.

"Look, Laney." He clawed back his dark hair. "It's been a long day. We're leaving for New Orleans tomorrow, and then we have the wedding the day after. I've had enough. I'm going to bed."

I'm going to bed. They hadn't seen each other for four days, and he wanted to go to bed alone. It was the first time he hadn't tried to touch her or lure her into bed with his wickedly seductive smile. Lure her to bed? He hadn't even bothered to kiss her hello!

Why? *Why?* Did it have something to do with Mimi du Plessis? Ugly suspicion choked her, and sick brittle fear. But whatever secret he held from her, it was too late to turn back now. She'd been innocent and stupid and naive. She'd jumped into bed, into love. And it had all led to this.

But she had to do the right thing. Just because he was unable to love her didn't give her the right to take away the one person he *could* love—their child.

"Wait," she said hoarsely.

"Fine." He looked at her wearily. "What do you want to tell me?"

She had tears in her eyes as she choked out the words that, just a few hours ago, had made her so happy. When she'd thought they had a future. When she hoped they were in love.

Looking at him with despair, she whispered, "I'm pregnant."

CHAPTER SIX

THE PILOT'S VOICE came respectfully over the intercom. "We've begun our descent into New Orleans, sir."

Finally. Rising to his feet, Kassius glanced across the plane's cabin, where his bride-to-be was huddled on a white leather sofa, as far away from him as possible. If Laney could have climbed out onto the edge of the wing to get a little farther away, he thought drily, she would have.

At least her nausea seemed to have improved. She'd only spent maybe an hour in the jet's bathroom. Other than that, in the hours since they'd left London, she'd been hunkered beneath that quilt, refusing to acknowledge his existence, though she managed to be friendly and polite to the flight attendant who brought her fresh water and saltine crackers.

Kassius ground his teeth.

Well, what had he expected? He'd chosen Laney because of her kind heart, her honesty and good nature. Of course, for her, love would be an expected part of marriage. She wasn't like Mimi du Plessis, who was coin-operated, motivated primarily by greed. Now that Mimi knew he wasn't pursuing her, she'd been frankly suspicious about his motives for quietly buying up all the loans and assets of her employer, Boris Kuznetsov. So he'd bought off those suspicions with an arrangement—she would be paid with gifts. The one she'd received yesterday had been particularly rich, a five-carat diamond necklace she'd seen advertised in an auction brochure that had supposedly once belonged to the Empress Josephine. He'd had it delivered to his house by a private courier earlier that week so he could give it to her.

But gifts, even expensive ones, wouldn't hold Mimi for long. Sooner or later, the woman would realize that there was more money to be made from blackmailing him and threatening to go to her boss. Mimi didn't know his true identity—no one did—but she could put Kuznetsov on his guard.

Kassius just needed a little more time. Boris Kuznetsov was overextended, overmortgaged and nearly out of assets. In a few months, he estimated, he'd be a broken man. All he had left was a shell of a company, now nearly stripped of assets, and the pink mansion on the Cap Ferrat. The one he'd promised to buy for Kassius's mother someday.

When he was a child, on all the nights he'd cried for his father when he was away, Emmaline had soothed Kassius to sleep with stories about the pink palace on the sea where someday they'd all live together. "We'll get that puppy you keep asking for, Cash, and eat your favorite meals. Every day will be like Christmas!" she'd said, and he'd believed her. He'd been comforted and had fallen asleep in the warmth of his mother's dreams.

But later, as a teenager, he stopped believing. By then, he hadn't seen or heard a word from his father for years, and he was getting into fights almost daily: with loudmouthed kids who sneered at him as a bastard or—far worse—called his sweet, softhearted, helpless mother a whore; and also with drunken neighbors who pounded their door at midnight, believing because they were poor and Emmaline "obviously slept around" that she was fair game, available either by payment or by force.

After his fights, his mother's face would be sad as she quietly washed his bloody knuckles, his ravaged cheekbones and, once, his broken nose. She tried to hug him and tell him the same stories about the future, when his daddy came back, how they'd all live together in that pink palace in the South of France. But he no longer believed in fairy tales, even if she did. His mother never quite gave up hope.

Not until the end.

Kassius's hands clenched, just thinking about it. Kuznetsov had indeed bought that pink palace by the sea, but only for himself, after Emmaline was long dead. And the man had held onto it, treasuring it over his other possessions. So that fanciful pink mansion would be the last thing Kassius would take. An ironic smile lifted his lips.

Funny to think that his child would be born around September, too. All his plans were working out with eerie precision.

Laney. Pregnant with his baby. He still couldn't quite believe it.

And tomorrow, they'd be wed. The thought made him feel strange and jittery inside. Why? Because he'd nearly succeeded? Because he'd gotten everything he wanted? The fortune. The power. The wife. The child.

An empire. A family.

Everything that had once been denied him. Everything...

Kassius looked at Laney. Everything but a bride who was willing to even look him in the face. Gritting his teeth, he walked over to her. "We're landing soon."

She peeked over the quilt, her expression cold. "I heard."

"You should buckle your seat belt."

"I did."

And she went back under the quilt.

So much for olive branches. Irritated, Kassius returned to his white leather swivel chair and buckled his seat belt.

Should he have lied to her last night? When she'd all but accused him of cheating on her with Mimi du Plessis, should he have looked into her stricken face and said those three little words that would have magically fixed everything? If he had, she'd have smiled at him in joy, and kissed him, and taken him with her to bed.

As it was, she'd slept in the guest room last night.

He folded his arms, feeling disgruntled and unfairly judged. He'd told her the truth. You'd think she would have sense enough to be grateful for that rather than being angry he hadn't tried to deceive her with pretty lies! But no.

She'd slept in the guest room, then given him the silent treatment. He didn't like it. But it fueled him with the one emotion he did feel comfortable with.

Anger.

When the plane landed at the small private airport outside New Orleans, Laney slipped into one of the designer outfits he'd bought her, still not meeting his gaze.

They came down the steps onto the tarmac, and he instantly felt hit by humidity and heat. "Where are we? The jungle?" he gasped, taking off his jacket, rolling up the sleeves of his button-down shirt.

"It's nearly March. Warmer than usual for Mardi Gras," Laney agreed, then looked at him coolly. "You're the one who needs to buckle in now."

She walked right past him, proud as a queen, to where their driver held open the door of the waiting Bentley.

Kassius stared after her. She looked magnificent in her sleek black day dress. She had no problem walking in stiletto heels now, and the expensive designer purse hung carelessly from her arm, as if she'd had expensive bags all her life, as if they were expendable. He suddenly missed the old Laney. This new one seemed hardened on the edges. He watched her climb into the back of the sedan without even a backward glance at him, much less a smile.

Once the driver and bodyguard transferred their luggage from the jet into the back of the sedan, they drove from the airport toward the outskirts of New Orleans, where her grandmother lived.

Kassius looked out the window. Laney was right. Even the air here smelled different. He rolled down his window, taking a deep breath. Even in late February, the air was swampy, humid and warm. But it was more than that. He took another breath, closing his eyes.

Exotic flowers overlaid the distant salt of the Gulf of Mexico and the muddy Mississippi. Beneath that, the faint scent of the bayou, of Spanish moss, of cypress and oak and a sweet, musky rot.

He'd never been to the American South. His visits to the United States had been limited to California and the Acela corridor between New York City and Washington, DC.

But his mother had been born here. He wondered what his life would have been like if she'd left Istanbul when Boris had first refused to marry her. What would have happened if she'd come back here, pregnant, to plead her case to her parents? If she'd given birth in New Orleans, if his grandparents had actually held him as a baby—would even they have truly been cold enough to refuse to let them stay?

He doubted it.

What would Kassius's life have been like if he'd grown up in a comfortable home, surrounded by family, always knowing he belonged?

If Emmaline had given up her romantic dreams of Boris and freed herself to find a man worthy of her love?

She might be alive now. Happy.

He could still hear the anguished echo of her voice. *If someone ever shows you the truth of who they are, if they lie or cheat or betray you, promise me you'll believe them the first time! Don't destroy your life, or your child's, wishing and hoping and pretending they'll change—*

Who would Kassius have become here?

Someone else. Someone different. Someone who knew how to love, maybe, he thought cynically. Everyone seemed to think giving one's heart away was a good thing. He didn't understand why—they only ended up broken.

Better to remain tough. The poverty and misery of his childhood hadn't destroyed him. To the contrary. The struggle had made him stronger. Able to risk anything. *Endure* anything.

He glanced at Laney sitting beside him.

He'd told her he knew everything about her from the private investigator, but that wasn't precisely true. He knew the basic facts of her life: birth, schooling, father's injury, mother's abandonment and later death. Those had been collated for him like bullet points on a résumé. But he was suddenly curious to know more than just plain facts.

"What was it like, growing up here?" he asked.

"It was fine." Laney's voice was cold, giving nothing away as she continued to stare out the opposite window.

She was blocking him out. He recognized the strategy. He did it all the time, and turnabout was fair play. He should shrug it off, let it go. But the fact that she'd been treating him so coldly for so many hours, in spite of her warm, generous nature, made him feel uneasy. Made him worry that makeup sex might not be enough to melt the ice.

Plus, he had something else to do first. Something he dreaded.

Meet her family.

The driver pulled up to a tiny, narrow house on a sagging street on the outskirts of the city. Not even the carefully tended flower beds could distract from the falling-down roof, the peeling screen door. There was pride here. But no money.

He saw Laney brace herself, take a deep breath, and put a big smile on her face before she climbed out of the car.

"Gran!" she cried, and a wizened, stout, gray-haired woman on the porch beamed and held open her arms.

She was much shorter than Laney and had to reach up to hug her granddaughter tight, patting her shoulders fiercely. She drew back, mystified. "What are you wearing, child?"

"Do you like it?" Laney twirled, showing the sleekly expensive black dress.

"Like it?" The older woman's mouth lifted humorously. "It's pretty enough, but honey, seeing all that black, all I can ask is, who died?"

Her grandmother turned her sharp gaze on Kassius, who'd followed Laney up the five steps to the porch. Craning back her neck, she looked him over critically, from his freshly shaven jawline—he'd shaved on the plane—to the rolled-up sleeves of his white shirt, his tailored vest and Italian shoes. Her gaze shifted to the luxury sedan at the curb, with the driver waiting inside it. Her black eyes clearly weighed his good sense and found it lacking. She sniffed. "You must be Kassius Black."

Kassius suddenly realized how ridiculous his car and driver were here. He glanced at Laney, hoping for some hint of how to proceed, but all he got was a similarly cold stare. Apparently both Henry women had a similar opinion of him at the moment.

Giving the elderly lady his best smile, he stuck out his hand. "You must be Yvonne Henry," he said smoothly. "I can see where Laney gets her good looks."

Mrs. Henry snorted, rolling her eyes. But she seemed to thaw out slightly. She started to reach out her hand. Then he made the mistake of adding, as he looked over the shabby house, "Didn't my business manager contact you? You were supposed to have access to all the money you need."

He heard Laney's intake of breath, saw Yvonne Henry narrow her eyes, drawing herself up to her full four feet eleven inches.

"Laney," she said coldly. "Please inform your boy-friend that we are not in habit of taking charity. Especially from strangers."

Had he been rude to offer them unlimited money? For a moment he was bewildered, then he realized Yvonne had taken his words as a slight on their home's appearance. Which he supposed it had been.

Yvonne Henry began watering the flowerpots on the porch. "Lunch is almost ready, but you'd best go introduce the man to your father first."

"I can't wait to taste your cooking," Kassius said, trying to dig himself out of the hole. "Laney said you're the best chef in the city. I haven't been able to think of anything else!"

"My cooking is what you're looking forward to? Not meeting us? Bless your heart." She turned to her granddaughter. "Laney May?"

"Let's go in," she said quickly, tugging on his arm.

"Nice to meet you, ma'am," he said politely and followed Laney into the house. When the screen door slammed behind him, he exhaled.

Laney was staring at him in disbelief. "You really aren't good at this."

"I think she likes me," he said.

Her expression changed. She glanced around them, drawing closer. "Just be respectful, okay?"

"What are you talking about?"

"My dad didn't like how you proposed to me, without asking his permission."

"Are you kidding? Who actually does that anymore?"

"Look around you," she bit out. "We're not rich jet-setters who are too full of our own importance to bother with the old values. We still believe in family. In love and respect."

Hmm. Kassius sensed criticism.

"So whatever you might think of me and my family," she continued, "can you please keep it to yourself and just pretend to be a decent person?"

Pretend?

"Fine," he bit out.

As Kassius followed her through the dark, shotgun-style one-story house, he noticed the damp walls and peeling wallpaper. He knew her father was in a wheelchair. Had there even been a ramp from the porch to the street? He wondered how her father managed to leave the house. If he did.

Kassius was going to be a father soon. He suddenly wondered how he'd feel if someone proposed marriage to his son or daughter on the other side of the world, without making the gesture of at least meeting the family first. Not good.

Pushing open a door, she led him into a dark bedroom. "Dad, I'm here!"

"Laney!"

She clicked on a light, and Kassius realized the man had been sitting in the dark. The bedroom was tidy and scrupulously clean. But the furniture was old, and the walls covered with photos of Laney at every age, often with a pretty, laughing woman he took to be her mother. The woman who'd abandoned them when they needed her most. Pictures Clark Henry could no longer even see.

"What are you doing in here, Dad, in the dark?" Laney said affectionately. She looked down at open book in his lap. In Braille. "Good book?"

Clark's unfocused gaze lit up in a smile. "Just waiting for you to get home! Come here, girl!"

Her face was tender as she went to him in the wheelchair and hugged him tight. "I missed you, Dad."

"Oh, sweetheart, it's been so long," Clark Henry said, blinking fast as he hugged her tight. When she pulled away, he cleared his throat. "And you're not alone."

"Did you hear me?" Kassius said awkwardly, feeling like an intruder.

The man smiled, but his expression was tight. "I could smell you at ten paces. Cologne and car leather."

Kassius gave himself a surreptitious sniff.

"Yes, Dad," Laney said. "This is my fiancé. Kassius."

"Pleased to meet you, sir." Taking the older man's hand, he shook it. He noticed Clark still wore his wedding ring.

"Nice firm grip," her father said and abruptly withdrew his hand. "But as for the fiancé business, we'll have to wait and see. I haven't decided if I'm willing to give you away."

"Dad, the wedding is tomorrow night!"

"If I don't give you away, there will be no wedding. So let me ask your fella a few questions." He glared in Kassius's direction. "What makes you worthy of my daughter?"

"Dad!"

"I'll take good care of her, sir."

"How?"

Kassius hid a smile. "I own many houses around the world, two jets, with a personal net worth of—"

"I get it. You're rich." Her father snorted, waving an impatient hand. "My daughter already told me, and so did that guy who kept calling, wanting to shove your money down our throats. That's not what I asked."

"Sir?" Kassius said, feeling bewildered again.

"What I *asked*," Clark Henry said, as if speaking to a not-so-bright child, "was how you are *worthy* of my *daughter*."

That brought Kassius up short.

He looked down at the man who'd lost everything in an oil rig explosion, trying to provide for his family. Working as a roughneck was hard, dangerous, isolating work—which was why it was well paid. But after the accident, the drilling company had found a legal loophole to deny compensation. Clark Henry had lost his sight, his mobility, his wife. Now he had no ability to work or even leave the house. He'd literally lost the power to look out for his family.

Kassius took a deep breath. And gave the only answer he could.

"I'm not," he said humbly. "But I intend to spend the rest of my life trying to make her happy. If you will please give me permission to marry your daughter."

The man's expression changed. He hadn't expected that. Nor, by the dumbfounded look on her face, had Laney.

Then with a cough, Clark frowned again. "Fine. You'll take care of her. But will you love her with all your heart? As my only child deserves to be loved?"

"Dad!"

"Let the man answer me, Laney May."

Kassius tried to think of what to say. Somehow he didn't think that his usual speech about "I'm just not a sentimental man" would satisfy Clark Henry. But he also had too much respect for the man to lie to him. He began, "The thing is..."

"Guess what?" Laney broke in, giving Kassius a warning glance. "I have news, Dad. Big news! The hugest! You need to come out into the kitchen so I can tell you and Gran at once."

"Good news?" her father said gruffly. "Or bad?"

"Definitely good." Laney kissed the top of her father's head. "But Gran will kill me if I don't tell you both. You go first, Dad."

Setting his jaw, her father pushed his wheelchair out of the bedroom, using his powerful arms to roll himself back down the long dark hallway. She started to follow him.

Kassius blocked her with his arm, putting his hand against the wall. He said in a low voice, "Thank you."

She stared at him for a moment, her deep brown eyes sad. "I didn't do it for you. I did it for them.

They want so badly for me to be happy. They can never know you…"

She didn't finish the sentence. She didn't have to. *You don't love me.*

Pushing his arm away, she left the bedroom. He followed her to the kitchen, where her grandmother was stirring a big pot on the stove.

Kassius took an appreciative sniff. "That smells fantastic."

"Oh, are you still here?" her grandmother replied, not bothering to look in his direction. Lifting her eyebrows, she glanced down at her son.

"I've decided to give the man a chance," Clark said gruffly.

"Really." She sounded skeptical. "Even after the way you were calling him a no-good—"

Clark coughed. "Laney said she has news."

Her grandmother paused in stirring the pot. "News? What news?"

Kassius looked at Laney. Now she was on the spot, her cheeks were pink. Clearing her throat, she said in an overly cheerful voice, "Kassius and I got a wedding present a few days early. We found out we're going to have a baby!"

Her grandmother's spoon dropped. "A baby!"

Clark turned toward Kassius with a blind scowl. "Baby?"

Kassius came behind Laney, putting his arms around her. He felt her trembling, though she gave her family a big smile. "Yes, a baby. And we couldn't be more delighted."

"A great-grandchild!" Yvonne breathed with delight. Then a shadow crossed her face. "But we'll never see the baby. You'll be living so far from us. We'll never see any of you."

"Just another member of the family he's taking from us," said Clark sourly.

Standing on the worn linoleum of the tiny, dimly lit, spotlessly clean kitchen, Kassius heard himself say, "Laney and I would be happy to have you stay with us. My jets are at your disposal. We have plenty of extra rooms. Please come and stay as often as you like."

Laney's jaw dropped.

Yvonne gasped, turning towards Clark, who had a stunned expression.

"I take it back." The elderly woman sniffed joyfully, wiping her eyes with her brightly colored apron. Coming up to Kassius, she stood on her tiptoes and enveloped both him and Laney in a hug. "Every bad thing I ever said. Because you're not just good people, Kassius—you're family!"

Later that night, Laney crept out of her childhood bedroom, with its pink ruffled comforter on her twin bed, foreign maps on the walls and overflowing bookshelves. Fresh from the shower, she was dressed in an old T-shirt and pajama pants as she sneaked down the hallway.

Engaged or not, pregnant or not, there were some rules that had to be followed in the Henry household, one of which was that an unmarried couple would never, ever be permitted to sleep in the same room. Even on the night before their wedding.

Too nervous to sleep, Laney had waited until her grandmother and father had gone to bed. Silently, she tiptoed down the long, dark hallway to the front room, where Kassius had been assigned to sleep on the sagging sofa.

Earlier that night, when her grandmother had handed him the pillow and blanket, Laney had half expected him to refuse and announce that he was off to a hotel. Instead, he'd just meekly said, "Thank you very much, ma'am."

Laney bit her lip. It wasn't the first time he'd surprised her today. She hadn't expected him to treat her family so well. As if he respected them. As if he really cared about their opinion. She was grateful but bewildered. Where was the arrogant man who claimed to have no feelings?

The front room was dark and empty, the pillow and blanket left in a pile on the sofa. Hearing a creak on the porch, she pushed open the peeling screen door.

Kassius was sitting on the old porch swing, his handsome face distant as he looked out into the dark night.

"What are you doing out here?"

He blinked, as if coming back to himself, and she wondered what he'd been thinking about. For answer, he just moved over, giving her a spot on the wooden swing.

She took a deep breath of the fragrant, cooling night air. She could hear the wind against the trees, the distant hum of city traffic. She could smell his expensive, woodsy cologne, the scent of cypress trees and musk.

"Not able to sleep, either?" she said.

"No."

She didn't want to ask if he was having wedding jitters like she was. "Is it the sofa?"

Kassius gave a wry smile. "It does have a hard spot right in the middle."

"I used to jump on it as a kid," she said apologetically. She bit her lip. "I feel guilty having a bed…"

"Don't," he cut her off. "I want you to have it. You need to be comfortable. How are you feeling?"

"Better. No nausea." She gave him a shy smile. "It might be because I'm home. Eating my grandma's cooking. I feel good. I feel…grateful." She looked at him in the shadowy night. A breeze blew the branches of trees across the nearest streetlight, moving light and shadow across his handsome, angular face. "Thank you for what you did today."

"I didn't do anything."

"You made my family love you."

He gave a low, cynical laugh. "By offering to give them use of my private jet? Or by not telling them the truth about my loveless heart?"

"You opened up your home to them. Home means family."

Kassius looked at her. In the dark, lowering sky, the crescent moon was haunted by a swirl of frosted cloud.

"How do you do it, Laney?" His voice was low and intense. "After everything that happened to you, how do you keep your heart open?"

"What do you mean?" she said with an awkward laugh. "Is there any other way?"

"Your mother abandoned you." His dark eyes seemed to burn through her. "She left your injured father and you and ran away with some boyfriend. It was monstrous…"

Laney sucked in her breath. "Don't say that! She made some mistakes, yes, bad ones, but—"

"Mistakes?" he said incredulously. "Abandoning a sick partner and a young, innocent child? It's beyond selfish. It was evil." His hands had tightened into fists, and his jaw seemed tight enough to snap. "She deserved to be punished…"

"She *was* punished," Laney said quietly. "She died. Of an overdose. Alone on a California beach, without my father or me around to help her and protect her from herself when she needed us most."

Kassius stared at her, then blinked, as if recollecting himself. He took a deep breath.

"How do you do it?" he repeated. He gestured toward the house. "All of you. After everything you've gone through, how can you still have such hope, such belief in love? Your father has clearly never gotten over her. He still has her pictures on his wall, pictures he can no longer see. He still wears his wedding ring!"

"You can't turn love on and off like a light when it's convenient," she said quietly. She stared down at the peeling finish on the wood porch. "I wish you could."

"You mean, you wish *you* could," Kassius said flatly. "Because you think you're in love with me."

Laney looked at him, astonished.

"But you're wrong." He shook his head. "You're not in love with me. You don't even know me."

For a moment, she didn't—couldn't—answer. Then

something about being here, in her own home in her own city, made her brave.

"There's a lot I don't know about you yet, that's true," she said quietly. "I don't know where you were born. I don't know your first language. I don't know why you gave Mimi those diamonds in secret, or why, for a man who worked so hard to create his fortune, you're willing to toss so much of it away on bad loans to her boss."

Folding his arms, Kassius set his jaw, looking away.

"But there are some things I do know." Laney tilted her head, looking at his silhouette in the moonlight. "I know you'll always be honest with me, even if that means saying things I don't want to hear. You're willing to commit your life to me, if not your heart. You have somehow already made my family love you. You're going to marry me tomorrow, and I know you will keep your vows to honor and cherish me. And I know above all that you will love our baby."

His eyes widened, and he turned toward her. For a long moment, they stared at each other in the moonlit Louisiana night, the only sound the creak of the chains on the porch swing and the soft whisper of the night breeze through the cypress and palm trees.

"Let me in, Kassius." Reaching out, she took his hand in her own. "Tell me your secret."

He stared at her for a long moment. Then, pulling back his hand, he abruptly rose to his feet.

"It's a busy day tomorrow. Get some rest."

And he left her on the dark porch.

CHAPTER SEVEN

STANDING AT THE altar of the two-hundred-year-old Gothic church, lit by candlelight on a dark February night in the heart of New Orleans, Kassius looked at Laney, radiant in her white dress.

"I now pronounce you man and wife," the minister intoned.

She looked like an angel, he thought. Her brown eyes glowed as she looked up at him. Her lips were full and pink, her dark hair pulled back beneath the long white veil. The wedding dress was vintage, with white lace sleeves and sweeping skirts.

The minister grinned. "You may now kiss the bride."

At last. Cupping Laney's cheek, Kassius lowered his head. He forgot about the hundred people watching from the pews and just kissed her. He felt her small body tremble. But her lips did not. She barely touched him before she pulled away. She was distant. Unreachable. Nothing like he'd expected from the warm, emotional woman he'd just married.

As Kassius drew back, suddenly he was the one who was trembling.

Around them, people were applauding and cheer-

ing from the pews, and a few threw rose petals as
Kassius took Laney's hand and led her back down
the aisle, past her openly weeping grandmother in the
fancy hat, and her father, who was still blinking back
tears from the experience of escorting his daughter
down the aisle.

The nave of the tiny, Gothic-style church was lav-
ishly decorated with expensive flowers and candles.
But the real heart of the ceremony had been the joy
of the wedding guests, mostly Laney's family and
friends. He'd only invited one real friend, his best
man, Spanish billionaire Ángel Velazquez. But that
was the difference between them, wasn't it? Kassius
had acquaintances, people he met for business dinners or a hedonistic week of skiing in Gstaad. He had
business allies and rivals, suck-ups and hangers-on,
all of whom he hadn't bothered to tell the wedding
planner to invite.

While Laney had family. She had friends.

Newly wed, the two of them walked out of the
stone church, and the wedding guests followed them
out into the warm, dark, moist Louisiana night, a
noisy, happy crowd, chattering, laughing, even bursting into song as they walked the short distance to
the reception, being held at an antebellum mansion
in the Garden District. The wedding planner, an ac-
complished woman, followed them with her headset,
making sure everything was ready for their arrival.

When Kassius saw the location of their reception,
he sucked in his breath. It was like seeing a ghost.

The mansion, set back from the street, looked exactly like his mother's childhood home. It had the
same type of old Spanish architecture, with covered

wrought-iron balconies. His mother's house had been built a hundred years later, two miles farther west, on St. Charles Avenue. He'd only seen it in photographs, before he'd had it destroyed.

A cold sweat broke out on his forehead, and his skin felt clammy beneath his tuxedo. He didn't know why this mansion, and the thought of a different house, was affecting him. The Cash house was in the past. Dead and gone. He'd never even gone to see the empty lot—that was how little it meant to him. So why did he suddenly feel dizzy?

He felt his bride's cool gaze on him as they walked past the wrought-iron gate, over a pretty path created by white rose petals and lit by white Chinese lanterns. He looked at her, and she instantly turned away to talk to a friend who'd come up beside her to squeal over her wedding dress, the beautiful ceremony, their future happiness.

And once they got inside the mansion, that was how the reception went, too. All night long, Laney offered bright smiles—fake! So fake!—to all of the people who loved her. For him alone—the one person on earth, it seemed, who did not love her—she offered coldness and a consistently averted gaze. As if she couldn't even bear to look at him.

And the ink was barely dry on their wedding certificate. Not a good sign.

To Kassius, the evening stretched on like torture, with an elegant sit-down dinner in the colorful high-ceilinged ballroom shimmering with lights. Gritting his teeth, he ate his dinner, barely tasting the blackened catfish or jambalaya. A tearfully happy wedding toast was offered by Laney's maid of honor, a childhood friend called Danielle Berly, now a married kindergarten teacher with two children. A much shorter, far less emotional toast was offered by his own best man, Ángel Velazquez.

He'd just held up his champagne flute and cried with a flourish, *"Buena suerte!"* Good luck. Which he obviously thought his old friend would need.

Kassius gritted his teeth and got through it. He smiled at all the right places and acted pleased when he and Laney cut the gorgeous six-tier wedding cake with its raspberry filling and white buttercream frosting with sugared flowers. He smiled for the photographer, leaning in toward his bride when she was refusing to touch him or look in his direction. When he took her out on the dance floor for their first dance together as a married couple, beneath the beaming smiles and oohs and aahs of her family and friends, he tried not to notice how she'd flinched when he'd touched her.

It didn't promise a very good honeymoon.

All he could think about was how different this night was from the New Year's Eve ball, when they'd first kissed and hadn't been able to keep their hands off each other. This wedding night should have been beautiful, and it had been, but coldly so, like a distant star. But why? What had changed?

With a sick feeling in his gut, he knew exactly why. Because she'd reached out to him last night, and he'd pushed her away.

He was tired of being alone. And weary, so weary, of having no one completely on his side.

Finally, at midnight, he'd had enough. She'd been visibly reluctant to depart, but he'd insisted. He'd finally taken her hand and led her out of the elegant old mansion to the circular driveway where a vintage Cadillac now waited, bedecked with sashes and white flowers.

Laney's footsteps slowed. "Where's the limo?"

"I decided it was too much."

"Really?" she drawled as the driver held open the back door. "Too much?"

Then she turned with a bright smile to wave at her family and friends who'd poured out of the mansion to bid them farewell. Kassius looked for Velazquez, but his friend was nowhere to be seen. He'd been such a hermit lately, Kassius was almost surprised the Spaniard had been willing to leave his half-million-acre Texas ranch to be his best man. Kassius certainly wasn't going to give him a hard time about ducking out early, but it meant only his bride's friends and family shouted and cheered after them as they departed, throwing white streamers at their car as they drove away.

Sitting beside his bride in the backseat, Kassius almost jumped when he heard loud bangs behind the car. Looking back, he saw rusty metal cans attached to the glossy bumper. He gave an incredulous snort. "I can't believe Ms. Dumaine—"

"The wedding planner didn't do those," Laney informed him. "I heard Gran giggling about it with the ladies of her bridge club."

The drive to the elegant hotel in the French Quarter where they were to have their honeymoon wasn't supposed to take long. Normally it would take fifteen minutes, the wedding planner had told him. But with the huge influx of tourists celebrating the week-end before Mardi Gras, traffic was heavy. The drive took forever.

Or maybe it just felt that way to Kassius, with the awkward silence in the backseat, the two of them not touching. Laney still wouldn't look at him and seemed more likely to strike up a conversation with the driver than the man she'd just pledged to honor and cherish.

Suddenly, he could stand it no longer. He leaned forward and spoke quietly to the driver, who nodded and changed the car's route.

"Why are we turning around?" Laney asked in confusion. The first words she'd spoken to him in ten minutes.

"You'll see," he said grimly.

The car turned back onto the wide, well-tended avenue, divided by tracks, for the historic St. Charles streetcar line. On both sides of the avenue were oak trees and gracious mansions, many at least a hundred years old.

"Here," he told the driver, and the man parked. Kassius abruptly got out.

It was past midnight now, and the street was quiet. This was a residential area, with a variety of architectural styles, from old Spanish to Greek Revival, Italianate to Colonial. Each mansion was evenly spaced with a large garden.

Except one house was missing, like a gap between teeth. He stood in front of the empty lot, stuffing his hands in his jacket pockets. Looking at a house he'd never seen.

Laney came up behind him. He heard the soft whisper of her skirts. "What are we doing here, Kassius?"

"You wanted to see the place I'm from?"

"So?"

Wordlessly, he pointed at the barren plot of land, lit up by a pale trickle of moonlight, ghostly and empty between the other elegant homes.

She stood beside him, looking at the lonely plot of land, nothing but overgrown grass and a single cypress tree. "You were born here?"

He shook his head. "My mother was." He looked at the empty lot. "This was her childhood home. She was the only child of the wealthy Cash family and ran off at nineteen to see the world rather than stay and marry the man they'd chosen for her."

A car drove past them on the quiet road, its lights illuminating Laney's big dark eyes.

"She fell in love with a Russian she met in Istanbul. She thought my father would marry her, but all he gave her was excuses. He floated in and out of our lives, promising he'd marry her soon, bringing us money and gifts. Until I turned eleven, and he disappeared completely." His jaw set as he looked out at the sad cypress in the moonlight, hearing the plaintive cry of night birds soaring invisibly above. "Later that year, my mother got sick. If we'd had money for proper medical care, she might have survived. As it was…it took her five years to die. Alone."

A lump rose in his throat. He didn't like the rawness of telling this story. He'd never told it to anyone before.

"But she wasn't alone," Laney whispered. Her hand reached for his. "She had you."

Kassius exhaled, almost shuddering with emotion. "When I was sixteen, as my mother lay dying, she wrote her parents and asked for help. She asked them to come see her, or at least to take me if she died. And they refused. *They refused.*"

He heard her gasp. He felt the warmth and softness of her hand as her fingers tightened protectively around his.

Turning away, he ground out, "This precious house meant everything to them. After they died, I bought it. Had it demolished." He gave her a crooked smile. "You know this is the first time I've seen this street?"

She stared at him. Reaching up, she stroked his cheek. Her dark eyes were luminous with unshed tears. "Oh, Kassius."

"That's why I changed my name. I didn't want my father's name. Or my grandparents'. So I chose my own. I bought a new birth certificate, new papers. I started a new life."

Standing on her tiptoes, Laney hugged him fiercely, and for a moment, he closed his eyes, accepting the comfort. He wasn't accustomed to it.

She drew back, looking up at him in her wedding dress, moonlight frosting her dark hair beneath the long white veil. "I know what it feels like," she said in a low voice. "To feel abandoned by family who is supposed to love you. That's what left the hole in your heart."

His voice was low and fierce. "Why don't you have one, Laney? Why? How can you still love like you do?"

"Because..." She blinked fast, then shook her head. "Because I still love my mother. I miss her. I try to remember the good times. Doing otherwise would bring me only misery."

Kassius stared at her, then shook his head.

"I feel differently," he said slowly. He looked at the bare plot of land. "Destroying this house was very satisfying. Looking at it now, I'm almost tempted to spit on the ashes."

"It won't bring you joy," she said in a small voice. "And it won't bring her back."

He looked at her sharply. For a moment, his heart was troubled. Then he steadied himself. Whatever Laney thought, he knew his plan for revenge against his father would make him happy. Very happy.

Crushing Boris Kuznetsov, taking his bankrupt business and the villa on the Cap Ferrat, would be the glory of Kassius's life.

"I'm sorry," Laney suddenly blurted out. Tears spilled over her lashes, and she wiped her eyes, trying to smile. "I was so angry with you. I ruined the most magical day of our lives."

With a low laugh, he took her in his arms.

"You didn't ruin it," he said softly. He gently wiped a tear off her cheek. "And a wedding is just one day. We'll have many magical days. A lifetime of them."

She gave him a grateful, watery smile, then a weak laugh escaped her. "This explains why you love Southern food. And why I felt like home to you." Her forehead furrowed. "So what was your name before? And how did you choose Kassius Black?"

He loved having her in his arms. He loved the way she was looking at him now. As if he were her hero again.

"When I was a child," he said slowly, "I liked hearing stories of ancient Rome. Kassius was the name of a Roman senator who raised an army to fight tyranny." He was also one of the conspirators who'd assassinated Julius Caesar, but he didn't elaborate. "And Black was how I vowed my heart would be."

Her eyes were shining. "Thank you for telling me."

"And now I need something from you." He looked down at her in his arms. "You know more about me now than anyone in the world. Promise you won't ask for more."

"But—"

His gaze held her. "Promise."

She sighed, looking sad. "All right. I promise."

He exhaled. He hadn't realized until then how tense he was. He felt horribly vulnerable. Exposed. But he also hadn't felt so close to anyone in a long time.

Laney was the one person he could trust. He suddenly knew she was the one person who would never betray him.

And he would always protect her, just as he would protect his child now growing inside her.

His child. The thought filled him with awe. He rested his hand against her gently curved belly. He would never make the mistakes of his father. He would be a good husband, a good father. Once his revenge was finished, he would leave the pain of his past in the rearview mirror. He'd spend the rest of his life focused on the future, on the present, always making sure that his wife and children were comfortable and warm and safe. They'd never have a single worry or fear. Those would be his jobs alone.

He looked down at Laney, pushing back a dark tendril of her hair. "You're my wife now. The mother of my coming child. The past is past. It's as your grandmother said. We are family. The future is what matters now."

"You're right," she whispered, and as he held her in the cooling night, she in her white dress, he in his tuxedo, their eyes met, and the air between them electrified.

"Mrs. Black," he said huskily. Lowering his head, he kissed her, tenderly at first, then with building need. In response, she wrapped her arms around him, drawing him down tighter against her.

Suddenly, all he could think about was ripping off her wedding dress. He wanted to forget. To be reborn in her. Inside her.

"Honeymoon," he growled, and pulled her toward the gleaming black Cadillac.

Laney felt the heat and weight of her husband's hard muscular body, barely restrained by the civilized tuxedo, as he pushed her into the car's backseat. The skirts of her white wedding dress plumped out like pillows as he savagely kissed her, pushing her against the smooth leather.

His fingers stroked through her chignon, causing long dark tendrils of hair to fall beneath her veil. His lips pressed against hers, causing her body to sizzle and ache from her fingertips to her toes and everywhere in between.

This was their true wedding, she thought as she kissed him. *This.* Where body met soul...

They barely made it to their luxury hotel, deep in the French Quarter, on famous Bourbon Street. It was lucky it wasn't far, and traffic had abated, or they might not have made it. They might have had their wedding night in the back of the vintage car with their driver in the front seat, fiddling with the radio and pretending not to notice.

When the car stopped, Kassius pulled her through the elegant lobby of the hotel, barely responding to the cheerful greetings of the employees and manager.

She breathed, "Don't we need to check in—"

"Everything is done."

Not everything, she thought hungrily.

As soon as they were in the elevator, he pressed the button for the third floor then pushed her back against the mirror and kissed her hard and hot. She barely heard the *ding* of the elevator door. He pulled her down the elegant, dimly lit hallway, then stopped in front of the door at the end. Pulling the key from his pocket, he opened the door and turned to her. Laney gasped as he lifted her up into his arms, her full white skirts and long white veil trailing behind them.

"You're mine now," he whispered. "Legally mine."

"Then you're mine," she murmured, twining her hands in his hair. "And I intend to use you exactly as I choose…"

Never taking his eyes from her, he carried her over the threshold. Kicking the door closed behind them, he set her down. She had only a brief glimpse of the large, elegant hotel suite and the gleaming neon lights of Bourbon Street visible through the French doors, which led to a covered wrought-iron balcony. He walked around her, staring at her wedding gown.

She blushed under his scrutiny. "Do you like it?" she said shyly. "It took forty-five minutes to get dressed, with all the buttons in back."

"If you think I'm going to wait forty-five minutes…" Reaching out, he ripped the back of her gown apart in a single violent movement, popping all the delicate buttons that held together the lace at the back.

She whirled around. "What are you—"

He spread the lace neckline wide, causing the seams to part, and pulled the dress straight down her body, leaving her standing in front of him wearing only a strapless white bra, a tiny lace G-string, a white garter belt holding up white fishnet stockings—and her long white veil.

"It was my grandmother's dress!" Laney cried indignantly.

"It was hers. Now it's yours. And what's yours—" Kassius's eyes were dark and smoldering as he roughly pulled her closer "—is mine."

A deep shiver went through her. Staring at his lips, she breathed, "You shouldn't have done it…"

"Like you said. The past is past. She had a long, happy marriage. And, starting tonight, so will we." He ran his fingers along the edge of her long white lace veil. "But you can keep this on," he said huskily. "I like it."

Picking her up, he tossed her onto the enormous bed, as if she were some kind of harem girl created exclusively for his pleasure. Two could play that game, she thought. Propping herself up on one arm, she reached out and grabbed the sleeve of his jacket.

"Take it off," she ordered.

He looked down at her in the shadowy bedroom of the hotel suite. Then he did as she bade.

"Now the tie," she said.

He undid the tie, dropping it the floor.

"Shirt."

He slowly unbuttoned his white shirt, then undid the cuffs. She had a vision of his hard-muscled chest, laced with dark hair, and the taut six-pack beneath. Her gaze lowered, her heart beating fast. She licked her lips.

"Trousers."

A sensual smile traced his lips as he looked at her with heavy-lidded eyes, then pulled off his black trousers and his boxers and socks in the bargain.

Her husband stood naked before her.

A deep shiver went through her as she saw his hard, naked body. His chest and shoulders were huge and muscular, tracing down to his trim, taut waist, and below that...

Holding her breath, mesmerized, she started to reach for him, wanting to wrap her hand around his huge, hard length, to cup and stroke and maybe even, if she dared, taste...

"Oh, no, you don't." His voice was low. "I followed your orders. Now you will follow mine." Leaning forward on the bed, he ran his fingertips up her leg, from the pale fishnet stocking to the garter on her bare thigh. "Take this off," he said huskily. "Take it all off."

Laney gave him a sensual smile. "As you wish."

Pulling the pins out of her chignon, she leaned back on her elbows and shook out her long, dark hair beneath the white bridal veil. She propped up one knee, exposing her bare inner thigh and the white garter, above the stocking.

His dark eyes widened as he looked her over. Her head was tilted back, her dark hair curling over her shoulders, her breasts—swollen from pregnancy—

thrust forward, barely contained beneath the sliver of strapless white silk bra.

He licked his lips. His gaze slowly traveled down her body, to the soft curve of her belly, to the spread of her hips. Her leg was propped up, revealing an expanse of bare thigh. His eyes traced down the white garters and tiny lace G-string to the see-through fishnets that started halfway down her thigh, all the way to her scarlet-painted toenails.

"Take it off," he repeated hoarsely.

She saw the hunger in his dark eyes, the way he took shallow breaths through parted lips. A thrill went through her.

"That's what I'm doing," she said innocently. "Taking it off."

And she was. Very, very slowly. Like a striptease to torture him. She wasn't sure what made her do it. Maybe it was the sudden realization of her power. Maybe she liked feeling his desire for her. Or maybe, just maybe, the fact of their marriage, of being his legal wife, gave her a confidence she'd never had before.

Still propped on her elbow on the bed, she stretched up her arm, fluffing up her long dark hair beneath the long white veil. She moved her hand slowly down, brushing her cheek, her neck, her clavicle. She moved it slowly over her full breasts, overflowing the flimsy white strapless bra, cupping one breast, pressing it against the other.

His eyes were nearly popping out of his head as he leaned against the bed, naked, not touching her. He said hoarsely, "What are you doing?"

"Oh." She looked up at him with big eyes, feigning surprise. "I guess I need to roll over to reach the clasp…"

And she did so, turning over on the bed, rolling on her tummy. Reaching back, she slowly undid her bra, causing it to fall off. Her full, swollen breasts spilled out in all their naked glory.

Tilting her head, she pretended to consider, placing one fingertip against her wet lips. "Hmm…" Kicking up her heels behind her, she twisted her head and looked back at her own backside, completely naked except for the straps of the white garter and the slender ribbon of the G-string. "Now what should I take off next?"

It was too much for her husband. With a low growl, he fell on her, turning her over so she was on her back. Without a word, he ripped off the white garter belt with two violent hands and did the same with the flimsy G-string. All she wore now was her veil, twisted behind her on the mattress, and her fishnet stockings, which now hung loosely on her legs, sliding down her thighs.

He pushed her back against the soft pillows and stroked his hand possessively down her body, between her breasts. "Tease me, will you?"

She fluttered her eyelashes coyly. "Must you keep ripping my clothes?"

"Not if you stay naked," he whispered, stroking her hair. Cupping her face, he kissed her.

His lips were rough at first, then gentled, became tender. The bristles of his chin were like sandpaper against her skin, but even that felt good to her. His hardness and roughness made her feel soft and feminine. His tongue teased hers as he deepened the kiss. Her naked breasts were crushed against his hard chest, and as her sensitive nipples rubbed against his muscled body, she nearly gasped with the sensation.

Moving, he slowly kissed down her body. Cupping her breasts, he lifted them in amazement. He could no longer fit a breast in his hand. He said in wonder, "You're so big."

"That's what you get for knocking me up."

He looked at her huge breasts and her belly, now with just the slightest hint of a curve, and his expression changed. A low hiss escaped through his teeth. He gently squeezed a nipple, lowering his head to the other. She felt the heat of his wet mouth on her, the stroke of his tongue, the nibble of his teeth, and this time she did gasp.

As he suckled her, he slowly moved his other hand down her body, to the gentle curve of her belly and farther still. He reached between her legs and she shuddered beneath him, swaying her hips. She could feel his hard shaft against her thigh. She wanted him inside her. Her nails tightened against his shoulder as she whispered, "Take me."

Pulling back, he looked down at her, and smiled. She realized he intended to refuse, to tease her and torture her with wanting, as she'd done to him. No way. Reaching between them, she stroked his length, and felt how rigid he was, straining hard against her. She felt him pulse in her hand. His dark eyes widened, then narrowed as he looked down at her.

"Now," she breathed, challenging him with her eyes.

A low growl from deep in his throat. Pulling back, he positioned himself between her legs. He pushed himself inside her with a single thrust, rough and deep.

Her lips parted in a joyful gasp as she felt him inside her, so hard and thick, filling her. Gripping her hips, he pulled back and thrust again. Her legs curled around his muscular backside, pulling him tighter into her. She moaned softly, and he increased the pace, riding her hard and fast, until the headboard was banging against the wall, increasing desperately in noise and rhythm. Beneath the impact and shake, the wedding veil that had been on the pillow suddenly flew up in the air, lifting on a puff of breeze. She felt pleasure build inside her, and she held her breath as it went higher…and higher…and higher still… She started to explode and heard herself scream. His low, triumphant shout joined with hers, and as he exploded inside her, the last thing she saw before she closed her eyes was the white lace veil, falling softly onto his back.

Moments passed before he opened his eyes. Rolling off her, he pulled her back against his chest, cuddling her into his arms. She nestled her cheek against his shoulder. He kissed the top of her head. "Wife."

"Husband," she whispered shyly. Her cheeks burned a little at the memory of how brazen she'd been. But he seemed to approve. He looked at her lazily beneath heavy-lidded eyes.

"It's just the start."

And so it was. If the wedding had been disappointing, because she'd been too mad at him to enjoy it, then their honeymoon, she would reflect later, was the most perfect, most romantic week of her life.

After they slept in each other's arms, they made

love again, then slept some more. When morning light came through the windows, they ordered breakfast in bed from room service, trays of waffles with powdered sugar and maple syrup, grits, fresh fruit, fried eggs with eye-watering red-hot pepper sauce, fresh-squeezed orange juice, and smooth chicory coffee with cream and sugar.

When Kassius accidentally got some powdered sugar on his cheek, she reached out and traced it lightly with her fingertips. "How did you get this scar, Kassius?"

His eyes darkened, then he gave a casual shrug. "It was a long time ago. Why?"

"You have powdered sugar on it. Kind of a mess."

"Ah." Touching his cheek, he looked at the sugar, then back at her. He lifted a dark eyebrow. "Don't mock. You have maple syrup on your chin."

"I do not!" she said indignantly, then licking her chin she discovered it was true. She heard the sudden catch of his breath.

"Let me help with that," he said huskily, and he leaned forward on the bed to lick it off her chin.

Seconds later, both breakfast trays crashed to the floor as he pushed her back against the bed, drizzling maple syrup all over her body, and she was smearing it on him, and they were licking and kissing every inch of each other. Afterward, they were seriously sticky and had to take a long, hot shower. Where they then discovered the sexy possibilities of having hot steamy water shooting all over their warm, wet, naked skin.

Laney couldn't get enough of him. And Kassius couldn't get enough of her.

After the shower, they toweled each other off and were tempted to get back into bed until they got a good look at the tangled sheets, sticky with syrup.

"Maid service," Kassius said breathlessly.

She brightened. "We'll go out!"

They let management know that maid service was required, then got dressed to venture out of the hotel. Laney was suddenly glad for the excuse. She was keen to show him her city—in a way, also his city— at the most thrilling time of the year. Mardi Gras.

Taking him by the hand, she led him out of the elegant formality of the hotel to the sheer madness that was Bourbon Street. It was barely noon, but crowds of people bedecked in over-the-top costumes or the Mardi Gras colors of purple, green and gold already filled the neon-lit bars and the sidewalks and streets. They walked around, gawking, then had lunch at a crowded courtyard restaurant, the best in the city. Since it didn't accept reservations, and Laney flatly refused to allow him to try to get bumped up the wait list by giving the hostess a thousand-dollar tip, they had to wait an hour to be seated. It was a novel experience for Kassius.

"I can't believe you want to wait for a table," he grumbled as they stood in the crowded outdoor bar. In the distance they could hear the music of a brass band over the noisy chatter of others waiting for a table.

"Anticipation is half the fun," Laney informed him.

Reaching out, he took her hand and tenderly kissed her palm, causing her to tremble. "Yes." His dark eyes smoldered as he straightened. "It is."

Laney stared at him, feeling hot and shivery all

over. Even though they were having fun wandering around, and even though Kassius had made love to her so many times already, she knew he was already counting down the minutes until he could get her back to the hotel. To his bed. And suddenly, so was she.

"Get you something?" the bartender said brusquely, clearly having no clue who Kassius was, treating him like just another rowdy reveler.

Kassius started to order his usual martini, but Laney interrupted him. "He'll have a hurricane. A sweet tea for me, please."

"Hurricane?" Kassius said with a frown.

"You'll see."

A few moments later, he was looking down with dismay at a garishly colored red-and-orange cocktail of rum and fruit juice in a large curved glass. "It looks like something a tourist would drink."

She sipped her own sweet, nonalcoholic iced tea. "How convenient, since you're a tourist."

"I don't like sugary things."

"You sure?" Her grin widened. Her eyelashes fluttered a little as she picked the glass off the bar and held it out toward him, her breasts pressing against him as she whispered, "Try it. You'll like it."

Never taking his eyes off her, he grabbed the glass and put his mouth on the straw. He gulped the whole thing down. Then he gasped, "I'd rather have some tart with my sugar…"

Then he kissed her, and she tasted the sweet tang of the orange juice and grenadine and rum on his lips.

After a lunch of Cajun-style cooking that Kassius raved about for hours, they ventured back outside. Bourbon Street had only gotten more crowded as the afternoon faded. A parade went down a nearby street and people went crazy as the floats went by, revelers waving in their sparkled costumes. Confetti and bead necklaces filled the air, along with noise and laughter and music.

As twilight fell, the French Quarter became so crowded it was almost impossible to walk through the streets. He held her hand tightly so as not to get separated.

"Let's have dinner back at the room," he growled, his palm pressing against hers, and she felt a zing of electricity through her body, an intense need that was overwhelming. Quivering, she nodded.

But as they hurried down a back alley, Laney heard shouting above them. She looked up to see three college boys on a covered wraparound wrought-iron balcony. They were hollering at her, shaking necklaces of beads. She blushed.

Kassius frowned and looked at them, then back at her.

"What do they want?"

She said meekly, "If I lift up my shirt and flash them my breasts, they'll throw me down some bead necklaces."

"Those bastards," he growled, his hand tightening over hers. "I'll go up there and teach them some manners…"

"It's not an insult. They mean it as a compliment— it's tradition."

Kassius looked both speechless and enraged.

Laney tilted her head as if considering. She tapped her chin. "Honestly, I could use some new jewelry…"

So it was that a half hour later, she found herself at

an exclusive jeweler's in the Vieux Carré, where he'd immediately dragged her and insisted on buying her a necklace of diamonds and sapphires that reminded her of that obscenely big sparkler in the movie *Titanic*.

"You can flash me later," he whispered in her ear, and she blushed and gave a laugh almost like a giggle.

She'd just been teasing him before, but as they walked the last blocks back to the hotel, Laney kept touching the cool platinum-set stones against her neck, thrilled that he was so determined to spoil her—in every way.

It was proof he cared. Wasn't it? And caring was almost like love. Wasn't that what such an irrational gift meant?

Then she remembered another diamond necklace, which he'd given to another woman in London. Her delight fled. The necklace suddenly felt like cold rock against her skin as she remembered her old boss Mimi, and Kassius's strange loans.

However it might seem right now, when they were married and taking such pleasure and joy in each other, Laney actually didn't know her husband at all. Yes, she knew where his mother had been born. But there was so much about him that was mysterious. She still had so many questions that now—with her promise—she couldn't even ask.

And how she wanted to know everything. She felt achingly close to him. Like she hadn't been a fool to picture him as noble and good. Like he might actually be that man.

If only he would share his past, share his secrets and heart with her!

But she feared he never would.

There are other ways to learn secrets. The poison-
ous thought crept into her mind. When they'd first
met, Kassius had hired a private investigator to dig
through her life. Before, she'd been furious at the in-
vasion of her privacy. Now she shuddered with the
temptation.

No, Laney told herself firmly. She wasn't going to
sneak behind his back. She would just love him, be
a good wife and pray that he would choose to open
up to her.

If she just loved him, sooner or later he would tell
her everything. Wouldn't he?

CHAPTER EIGHT

EXCEPT, OF COURSE, he didn't.

Six months later, Laney was trembling as she pressed her phone tighter to her ear. "What did you say?"

"Your husband's real name is Cash Kuznetsov," the investigator said.

Laney's heart was pounding as she sank into a chair in their new Monaco flat. With a deep breath, she rubbed her enormous belly. She'd hoped it wouldn't come to this. Hoped that over the course of their marriage, her husband would just reveal his secrets to her of his own free will.

But he hadn't. And as they'd traveled frequently around the world, in some ways—in spite of his generosity with his wealth, his care of her family and of her—he'd been more secretive than ever.

Last week, she'd discovered him out of bed in the middle of the night in their new Monaco home. Apparently, the villa on Cap Ferrat that he'd been hoping to buy for the last six months was still not on the market. So in a fit of pique, Kassius had purchased a bigger penthouse in a luxury high-rise, five bedrooms with a rooftop terrace and panoramic view of

Fontvieille Harbor, the rocks and the sea. She was still in shock that he'd make a thirty-million-euro purchase on impulse. As a temporary replacement for the house he *really* wanted.

That villa on Cap Ferrat must really be something, she thought in awe.

That night, she'd discovered her husband pacing as he spoke quietly into the phone. When she'd confronted him, asking him whom he could be speaking with at two in the morning, he'd refused to explain. "If you don't want me to lie, you promised never to ask," was his terse response.

It had been the last straw.

The next morning, feeling hurt and anxious and twisted up with emotion, she'd contacted a private investigator recommended to her by Kassius's friend, the best man at his wedding, Ángel Velazquez. The Spaniard billionaire was the only person she knew who wouldn't be afraid to go against Kassius Black.

Ángel had been amused when he'd gotten her call. "You already wish to hire a detective, after just a few months?" he'd said sardonically. "How pleasant marriage must be."

She'd gone hot with embarrassment and tried to stammer out excuses before he'd mercifully cut her off. But at least he'd given her the name of a very good private investigator, who liked the idea of a challenge—of discovering the true background of the man whom no one else had ever been able to properly trace. He'd told her, "I just need a place to start."

Feeling like a traitor, Laney had given him the address of the Cash home on St. Charles Avenue—the address where Kassius had recently decided to build a brand-new house expressly for her grandmother and father, with a guest wing where she and Kassius could visit after the baby was born.

Just thinking of how she'd gone behind his back while he was building a house for her family made her feel ashamed.

And he'd done far more for the Henry family than just the house. Since the marriage, Laney's grandmother and father now considered Kassius family. So they were happy to let him spend money on them. They didn't see his generosity as charity, but merely as his way of showing love.

"Some men just aren't good with words, Laney May," her father had explained.

"Any man that's a man," her grandmother grumbled.

So they hadn't fought Kassius when he'd insisted on sending Clark to Atlanta on his private jet to see a highly regarded doctor who offered innovative medical treatments. Especially after Kassius had explained his anguish that he'd been unable to get the best care for his own mother when he was young.

Only a heart of stone could have refused him, and Clark Henry, beneath his gruff exterior, had no heart of stone. After months of treatment, her father was seeing improvements, with partial sight already restored in one eye.

"There's this nurse with a really sexy voice who's been taking care of me. I'm just trying to get a good look at her," he'd explained half-jokingly, but he'd sounded happier than Laney had heard him in years.

As if her father having hope and a new crush wasn't enough, her grandmother had been traveling the world. Yvonne started with a ten-day cruise of the eastern Caribbean, but the day she'd returned, she'd hopped on a new ship to see the western side. In the last six months, the longtime widow had cruised the whole world, meeting new friends and even a few new boyfriends.

"You've left a trail of broken hearts across the world," Laney liked to tease her.

Yvonne just said coyly, "I can't help it if men keep falling for me." Her grandmother had now branched out to even greater adventures, backpacking across Europe, staying at hostels, and most recently visiting Angkor Wat in Cambodia with a Norwegian man friend ten years younger.

Laney was incredibly touched and grateful for what Kassius had done for them—all of them. She'd tried to be satisfied. She'd reminded herself that Kassius was a good husband and would be a good father. She'd told herself that every man had secrets.

But she couldn't let it go. And now she understood why.

"What's his father's name?" she whispered now, but as the investigator told her, she'd already known what it would be. By the time she hung up the phone, all the pieces were clicking into place. The loans he'd made to a man who was unlikely to ever repay. The secret gifts to Mimi du Plessis.

Laney thought of the hard light in his eyes the night of their wedding, when he'd shown her the empty land where his grandparents' elegant mansion used to be. *This precious house meant everything to them. After they died, I bought it. Had it demolished.* It was the only thing that made sense.

She knew why he kept coming back to Monaco and what he was after. And why.

Laney paced through the afternoon, waiting for Kassius to come home. When he finally did, it was hours later. She was sitting wearily by the wide windows overlooking the sparkling lights of the city in the dark night, and the dark sea beyond.

Kassius frowned at her, obviously shocked to find her awake so late, with a bottle of scotch on the table beside her.

"You're drinking scotch?" he said in disbelief.

Well might he be surprised—she hadn't had even a sip of champagne since she'd discovered she was pregnant. Opening the bottle, she poured some in a short crystal glass. "It's not for me." She held out the glass. "It's for you."

Setting down his laptop bag, he looked at her with a frown and slowly took the glass.

"I know who you are, Kassius," Laney said quietly, looking up at him from the sofa. "And I know who your father is."

He took a small sip of scotch, watching her. "Do you?"

Exhaling, she nodded. "All this time, I've wondered about your expensive gifts to Mimi du Plessis and your endless anonymous loans to her boss. Now I understand. You didn't want her to tell Boris Kuznetsov all those loans were from the same source—you. You didn't want him to get curious about you. Because if he looked at you too closely, he might recognize you as the eleven-year-old boy he abandoned in Istanbul. Cash Kuznetsov, the illegitimate son of Boris Kuznetsov and Emmaline Cash."

"How did you learn this?"

"An investigator. I got his name from Ángel Velazquez."

For a long moment, Kassius looked at her, then he barked a laugh. Lifting the glass, he drank all the scotch in a single gulp. He set the glass down with a clunk.

"Fine," he said abruptly. "You got me."

"What are you trying to do to him?" she whispered, hoping against hope she was wrong.

He poured himself another glass of scotch, then considered her. "Destroy him, of course."

"How?"

His sensual lips curved in a bitter smile. "Like I told you, Kuznetsov wasn't around much when I was growing up. He was a busy man, working in Moscow, and had to do lots of travel throughout the Soviet Union and beyond. That was how they'd met, when she was a stewardess based out of Istanbul." He took another sip of scotch. "After he abandoned us, after my mother got sick, I went through her papers and found his address in Moscow. I wrote letters. He never replied. When I was sixteen, I hopped a train to Moscow and found out why. *He was already married.*"

"Oh, no," she breathed.

He shrugged. "I saw him walking, arm in arm, with his beautiful blond wife in her fancy clothes, into a mansion, followed by three golden retrievers bounding at their heels. So cozy. So rich. So happy."

Laney sucked in her breath.

"I was so shocked I stumbled back. Straight into a metal fence. That's how I got this." He traced the raised white scar on his cheekbone. His lips twisted. "He'd strung my mother along for sixteen years, promising her he'd marry her someday and buy her a candy-pink villa in the South of France. I still remember how happy those dreams made her. She always believed he was coming back to her. I didn't have the heart to tell my mother what kind of man he really was."

Laney suddenly understood so much. "No wonder you hate the idea of love," she whispered brokenly. "To you, all it means is a lie."

His jaw clenched, and he looked away, toward the vast darkness of the sea.

"I didn't want you to know, Laney," he said heavily. "Because it's not your way. I wanted you to keep your ideals about love. About me," he added quietly.

She slowly rose from the sofa. At eight months pregnant, she had to push herself up with a little more force than in the past.

Grabbing his hand, she placed it over the spot on her belly, where she felt her baby kicking inside her.

"That's our son," she said in a low voice. His eyes went wide.

"Son?" he breathed.

She smiled bashfully. "I know we promised each other we would wait to find out, but well... I couldn't help myself from asking at my last appointment."

"A son." He blinked fast. "Perfect. I've already got my hands on what's left of his company. All he has left now is the villa. If he takes one more loan, I will have that, too."

Pain ripped through her. "Don't do this. Revenge won't make you happier. It won't. Please, just let it go!"

"Let it go?" He stared at her incredulously. "He has to be punished for what he did."

"Please," she whispered. "For my sake. For our baby's. Just talk to him. There might be extenuating circumstances. You don't know."

His eyes hardened. "I know enough."

"Listen…" Her voice cracked. "I was angry all the time when I was a teenager, hating my mother for leaving us, blaming her for dumping everything on us so she could run off and be free. But I was so unhappy. So awfully unhappy. I didn't want to feel that way. So I decided to forgive her. To remember the good times. I chose love—which is what I feel for you, Kassius." She took a deep breath and lifted her gaze to his. "I love you."

His expression looked frozen. "You love me?" he said in a low voice. "After everything I told you?"

"You're a good man. I know it." She put her hand over his as their baby kicked again. "Don't hurt your father. Our child's grandfather."

He pulled back his hand, looking angry. "You care so much about the man?"

"I care about you. And our baby. And what this revenge will mean for us—all of us."

His sensual mouth curved. "You're part of it, Laney."

"Me?"

"It was always part of my plan. A beautiful family, a wife, a child. Kuznetsov's wife divorced him for another man long ago. He has no other children. After I take his villa and tell him who I am and why I've ruined him, he'll know he's lost every chance at happiness he might have had. Including his only family who might have loved him. His own grand-children will never know his name."

Laney stared at him in shock.

"No wonder you wanted to marry me," she said numbly, feeling heartsick. "No wonder you were so determined from the first night to get me pregnant. I thought it was love at first sight. But for you, it was only revenge…"

Reaching down, he put his hand on her shoulder. "Not only that. Not anymore. I've come to trust you, Laney. That's why I'm telling you the truth."

Great, she thought bitterly. *Now* he was trusting her.

Her eyes narrowed as she shook her head. "If you're not going to try to talk to him, I will—"

Kassius's expression changed in an instant. He grasped her shoulders tightly, looking down at her with a ferocity she'd never imagined. "If you even think of telling Kuznetsov, you are dead to me, do you understand? I will never see you again. Neither you nor the baby."

Shocked, she searched his gaze.

"I don't believe you," she said slowly.

"Don't you?" His jaw set. "I think you do. If you betray me, I will divorce you, Laney. I will start new. Find another woman. Have a different child."

His grip tightened. "You're hurting me!"

He released her. She rubbed her arm, feeling hurt and bewildered by the savage change in him.

"I have to trust you, Laney." Kassius looked at her for a long moment, a mixture of emotions crossing his face. When she didn't answer, he grabbed his laptop bag and left the penthouse without another word. The front door closed with a bang.

But it wasn't her arm he had injured. It was her heart.

She stared after him, filled with despair. Walking around the enormous five-bedroom luxury flat, with its wide windows overlooking the sea and harbor, she felt alone, aimless and lost.

Laney stopped in the doorway of the cheerful nursery she'd decorated for their baby. She'd been so happy when she'd gotten Kassius to put up the goofy giraffe on the wall. She'd convinced herself that he was starting to open up to her. To care.

If you even think of telling Kuznetsov, you are dead to me, do you understand? I will never see you again. Neither you nor the baby. If you betray me, I will divorce you, Laney. I will start new. Find another woman. Have a different child.

He didn't love her. To him, she was interchangeable. Any woman would do. Any child. All he needed was window dressing for his revenge.

Fury and despair coursed through her, and without thinking, she grabbed the giraffe decoration and ripped it half off the wall with a cry. Then she saw what she'd done, and she collapsed into sobs, covering her face with her hands as she fell on her knees to the brightly colored rug.

All a lie. All something she'd done to convince herself that Kassius could change.

He couldn't. He didn't even want to.

Kassius was destroying his own soul, and she was helpless to save him.

She cried herself to sleep. At dawn—sunrise came

early in late August—she found Kassius's side of the bed hadn't been slept in. Hadn't he come home last night? She crept downstairs and saw his laptop bag outside his home office. She peeked in the open door and saw him sleeping fitfully on the black leather sofa. She exhaled.

She was starting to push open the door to talk to him, then stopped. What was the point? He was so lost in his childhood grief and rage that he'd spent a lifetime planning his revenge. He didn't see how destructive it was. Whether or not Boris Kuznetsov deserved punishment for what he'd done so long ago, Laney felt with all her heart that her own baby deserved a father who knew how to love. How to forgive.

But Kassius was so lost in his anger, telling him that was a waste of time.

Laney's eyes suddenly narrowed.

If only she could just get the two men to talk, face-to-face. That was the answer—it was always the answer. Maybe the problems wouldn't be solved, but it had to be more satisfying than all this sneaking around, grudge holding, revenge. They had to talk and get this in the open.

She recalled the stark look in Kassius's dark eyes as he'd said, *I will never see you again. Neither you nor the baby.* For a moment, fear gripped her.

She looked down at her belly, putting her hand protectively over her baby. She was only three and a half weeks from her due date. She thought of the risk she would take, trembling between love and fear.

But her life had taught her to choose love. Wasn't that worth the risk? She had to try to save him as she hadn't been able to save her mother. She was the only one who could. She told herself that his words had been spoken in anger, to try to control her actions. Kassius was too good a man to actually desert her, and especially not their baby.

As Mrs. Beresford—who had volunteered to come here from London to look after them—made breakfast, Laney took a long shower and then got dressed in a simple cotton sundress and sandals. As she ate scrambled eggs, croissants and fruit at the dining table, her stomach fluttered with nerves as she looked up Boris Kuznetsov's address.

By late morning, when Kassius still hadn't left his home office to talk to her, she realized he was probably on the phone wrapping up the final loan right now and preparing with his accountants and attorneys to move in for the kill. It was now or never. She made her decision.

Going down to the garage, she discovered Benito conversing with the driver as he waxed the limo. They both snapped to attention when they saw her.

"Do you need me to drive you somewhere, madame?" he asked respectfully. She backed away.

"Um, no…" She saw the key to the sports car hanging in the open wall safe and snatched it up. "I'm just running a quick errand."

"Monsieur Black prefers that I drive you…"

There was no way she was going to risk him finding out where she was going. Not before this silly business was settled and smoothed over. "Thank you, but it's not necessary," she stammered. "It's just a little thing, and I want to surprise my husband."

She thought of how surprised he'd be. But first,

she had to get into the sports car. With her big belly, the low-slung seat was a tight squeeze, and very low to the ground. Once in, she wondered if she'd ever be able to get out again.

"All right, madame?"

"Absolutely." Swallowing, trying not to be nervous, Laney started the engine, automatically turning the air-conditioning on full blast. Even with the coast's cooling sea breezes, August in Monaco felt uncomfortably hot to her at her advanced state of pregnancy. She'd gained thirty pounds, plus the growing baby felt like her own personal furnace. The blast of cool air was welcome as she also rolled down the windows and drove the tight, curvy coastal road west, over the border into France.

Her hands were shaking as a half hour later, she turned onto Cap Ferrat, the famously beautiful green peninsula jutting out into the shining blue Mediterranean, one of the most expensive residential areas in the world. It was filled with gated villas owned by famous people, from tech billionaires to rock royalty. She passed a few guarded gates before she reached the right one. She stopped at the gatehouse.

"Madame?" the guard said respectfully.

Laney licked her lips awkwardly. "I'd like to see Mr. Kuznetsov," she blurted out. "He's not expecting me. Please tell me that I'm the wife of Kassius Black, and I bring news of his son."

The guard turned back into his guardhouse, and made a quick call. He returned looking stern. "He says he has no son, madame."

"I'm speaking of the son he abandoned in Istanbul."

The guard spoke quietly again, and when he

turned back to face her, his expression was wide-eyed. "You're to go in at once, if you please."

Laney drove through the gate, passing overgrown gardens before entering a courtyard. Behind the big stone fountain was the entryway to the villa, which was big, pink and gaudy, with an amazing view of the sea behind it.

She parked the black sports car in the courtyard, next to a shiny red convertible with a Monaco license plate. She turned off the engine. The flowering trees and brilliant bougainvillea were a riot of color, but she noticed the garden seemed strangely overgrown, almost entirely wild, as if no gardeners had touched it for months.

She was doing the right thing, wasn't she? Laney's hands tightened on the steering wheel as she took a deep breath. Right or wrong, it was too late to turn back. She had to take courage for what lay ahead.

She felt ungainly as an elephant climbing out of the low-slung sports car. Especially when she saw the slender, well-dressed blonde who'd just come out of the mansion. Her lips parted in shock.

It was Mimi du Plessis, her old boss, the American-born Comtesse de Fourcil.

When she saw Laney, her red lips curled.

"If it isn't my former employee. Now the glamorous Madame Black." Coming closer, Mimi looked her over contemptuously. "You really think you've won it all, don't you, Laney? You think he will love you. He won't. You're nothing but a broodmare." She patted the glossy red convertible. "Do you like it?" She smiled viciously. "Your husband had it delivered for me this morning."

That explained the midnight call Kassius hadn't wanted to explain. Laney blessed her investigator. Otherwise, she'd have believed her husband to be unfaithful and been devastated. As it was, she lifted her chin defiantly.

"I know all about it," Laney said. She tilted her head as she faced her old boss. "So what was he paying you for this time? Was it the final payoff for facilitating his very last loan to your boss?"

Mimi looked disappointed. Tossing her blond mane, she said spitefully, "Much good it will do him now. I brought all the paperwork for the loan, but Mr. Kuznetsov was suspicious about why anyone would lend him money now, when his company is bankrupt, or why I would choose to help him when he's had to let all his employees go. The game is up. Nothing left for me now but to find some wrinkled old rich man to marry." She sighed. "But I told him what he wanted to know. All the loans he's taken over the last two years have secretly been from the same man—Kassius Black." Her smile widened. "So all the gifts your husband gave me were for *nothing*. He's still busted."

Laney stared at her old boss, this beautiful, empty woman, divorced four times, who cared about nothing and no one. "I feel sorry for you," she said quietly.

Mimi's eyes blazed, then she gave a brittle laugh. "Sorry for me? Don't be ridiculous. Everyone wants to be me."

Climbing into her gorgeous red convertible, the comtesse adjusted the mirrors and drove away from the pink villa with a squeal of tires and a cloud of dust that left Laney coughing.

"Madame Black."

Looking up, she saw an older man, trim and well dressed, with salt-and-pepper hair, waiting anxiously by the front door. Recognizing him, she came toward him, smiling, and extended her hand. "Thank you for seeing me."

He shook her hand, then motioned for her to follow him inside.

Laney walked through the villa, which was oddly sparse of furniture. She saw rectangles on the walls where the wallpaper was suspiciously bright. He saw her glance, and gave a rueful smile.

"I've had to sell off a few unnecessary things. Like paintings." He looked at her, and added kindly, "And turn off the air-conditioning, I'm afraid." That explained why the villa felt so uncomfortably hot.

He escorted her into a large sitting room, empty except for a few antique cushioned chairs and a table. A breeze came from the open windows overlooking the sea. "Would you care for some tea, Mrs. Black?"

"Thank you."

"I hope it's not too strong." He poured her a cup of tea from a small electric samovar. "I'm out of practice at this. I used to have servants, but I've had to let them go. Along with all my other employees."

"That must have been hard."

His expression sagged. "My company just couldn't compete with all the cheaper supplies flooding the market. Other than my security guard who keeps thieves and reporters away, I have only my housekeeper left, but she's too old and frail to work. She just has nowhere else to go. Kind of like me." He looked wistfully around the elegant, half-empty salon. "I have just this villa left, but soon this, too, will go."

He paused, sitting in the chair across from her. Then he leaned forward, his dark eyes burning through her, reminding her so much of Kassius's. She thought he would ask her about Kassius's loans. But he didn't.

"Now. You said you have news of my son?" he said anxiously. "My Cash? He's alive?"

Laney took a deep breath.

"Yes," she whispered. "Very alive. And close."

Emotions crossed the man's face painfully. "How do you know this?"

Laney looked at him, her heart pounding in her throat. She prayed she was doing the right thing that would save their family, not destroy it.

Setting down her tea, she said quietly, "Because I'm married to him."

"Mrs. Black is on the house phone for you, sir."

Kassius looked up from his laptop with a frown to see Mrs. Beresford in his doorway. Sitting at his dark lacquered desk in his home office, with its view of the sea, he was simultaneously going through the numbers for the potential development of a ten-story residential building in London and holding his cell phone with his shoulder as he spoke with his head contractor on the new stadium being built in Singapore. He covered his phone with one hand. "She's calling me from the bedroom?"

"No, sir. From your father's house. She said you weren't answering your mobile."

It took two seconds for that to sink in. He said tersely into the phone, "I'll call you back." Pressing his hands against the desk, he rose furiously and took the cordless receiver from his housekeeper's hand. Electricity was making his nerve endings vibrate and hum with something he hadn't felt in a long time— fear. "Laney?"

"Kassius, don't hate me," her sweet voice pleaded. "I had to do this. For you. I'm with Boris Kuznetsov and I've told him everything. Who you are, the loans, how you got your scar in Moscow. Everything. We're drinking tea in his parlor."

It was like being punched in the gut. Harder than he'd ever been punched in his life. His knees went weak as he felt the work of a lifetime undone by a woman's betrayal.

Not just any woman. His wife.

Not just any wife. The mother of his soon-to-be-born son.

If you even think of telling Kuznetsov, you are dead to me, do you understand? I will never see you again. Neither you nor the baby.

He'd told her what would happen. He'd *told* her.

"I'll be there as soon as I can," Kassius said tightly and hung up. But for a moment, he continued to grip the phone, so tight that the plastic receiver started to crack beneath his fingers. His eyes stung as he realized what Laney's naive, reckless action had just cost them all.

He closed his eyes, leaning his head against the receiver. He hadn't cried in years, but when he opened his eyes again, they were watery.

He'd just lost everything.

The dream of his past—of getting his revenge.

The dream of his future with her—of their family.

Laney had thought she knew better. Thought she

could cure him with her ridiculous beliefs about love. Her foolish idealism had just cost him everything he cared about.

He'd trusted her.

And this was the result.

If someone ever shows you the truth of who they are, if they lie or cheat or betray you, promise me you'll believe them the first time! Don't destroy your life, or your child's, wishing and hoping and pretending they'll change.

Kassius felt the phone crack beneath his grip. Tossing it down across his lacquered desk, he looked for his car keys. He went down to the garage and saw the sports car was gone. Laney, with her laughable driving skills, had taken his favorite car on her way to betray him. Of course she had.

"Benito," he called tightly to his bodyguard. "Have Lamont pull the limo around."

Perhaps it was better this way. Better for him to bring his bodyguard and driver so his wife could immediately face the price of her betrayal.

Kassius looked out bleakly at the sunlit Mediterranean as the driver, with his bodyguard in the front seat beside him, twisted the tight curves of the slender cliff road. The driver pounded on the brakes when a car wove briefly into their lane, and loud French curses came from the front seat. Kassius barely noticed as he took a phone call from his business manager.

Hanging up a few moments later, Kassius looked out the window. He felt weary. He felt dead. His hand tightened. The damage was done.

The car drove up to the guardhouse at Kuznetsov's gate and was almost instantly waved through.

"Stay here," he ordered his men after the limo was parked. "You know what to do."

The driver nodded and reached for something in his jacket that looked like a flask. "Just juice," he said in response to Kassius's frown.

"Benito?" he demanded.

"Got it." His bodyguard looked mutinous, but then, he'd come to respect and admire his boss's wife. Everyone had.

Kassius's soul felt hollow as he looked up at the ostentatious pink villa, the villa that he'd intended to take for his own and throw the former owner into the gutter to starve, as he'd left Kassius and his mother so long ago. A lump rose in his throat.

He'd already heard from his business manager that his father had canceled the last pending loan. Kassius could take possession of all the other homes Boris Kuznetsov had signed over as collateral. But who cared about those? This—he looked up with a sharp pain in his throat—this pink mansion, made of spun sugar and fairy-tale dreams, was the only one that mattered. And he'd failed, through no fault of his own.

That was a lie. It was *entirely* his fault, for trusting Laney. For letting himself be vulnerable to her. If he hadn't taken her to his mother's childhood home the night of their wedding, it was unlikely any private investigator could have made the connection. He'd covered his tracks too well. He'd been careful.

Until Laney had gotten under his skin and left him open for attack.

He walked up to the front door, which opened before he could knock. A tiny elderly woman, nearly bent over with osteoporosis, motioned to the right hall. "They're in the salon, monsieur," she said grandly in French. "I'll show you the way…"

But seeing how she hobbled painfully in front of him, he said hastily, "No, *merci*, I can easily find my own way, madame."

Tossing him a grateful look, she gave a nod. Kassius walked down the empty hallway to a high-ceilinged, elegant room in cream and pale blue, with sparse antique furniture and walls devoid of decoration. And at the center of it all, his traitorous dark-haired wife sat at a small table with the man who'd destroyed Kassius's childhood and driven his mother into an early grave, the two of them cozily drinking tea from an electric samovar.

"Kassius!" his wife exclaimed, rising to her feet and coming forward, holding out her hands to him as if she expected an embrace, as if she expected him to thank her for destroying his life. It was cruel, he thought, that she'd never looked more beautiful than now, even dressed in a plain sundress and sandals. With her lush breasts and belly, and the sparkle in her brown eyes and bounce in her dark hair, she was loving and warm. Laney Henry Black was everything he'd ever wanted in a wife.

Everything he should have known would ultimately destroy him.

"Laney," he responded coldly, not touching her. He turned his attention to the older man who'd risen from the chair beside her. His face was haggard and pale, and he was staring at Kassius with stricken dark eyes exactly like his own.

"Is it true?" Boris Kuznetsov whispered, looking at him searchingly. "You're my son?" He choked out, "My little Cash? Can it really be?"

Cash. A blast of memory went through Kassius like the heat of a fiery explosion. No one had called him that in a long, long time.

All his years as a child, he'd yearned for his father's acknowledgment, his acceptance. Just his presence. And now, at last, they were in the same room, but now Kassius no longer wanted anything from him—but justice.

"It's true, old man." Turning to Laney, Kassius said blandly, "Why don't you wait outside?"

"Really?" Her forehead crinkled uncertainly.

"My father and I have much to discuss."

Laney bit her lip. "If you're sure—"

"I'm sure."

She looked up at him anxiously. "Please don't be mad at me for this," she said. "I know you didn't want me to tell him, but it was the only way to save you from making a horrible mistake."

"I understand." And he did. Laney being who she was, she'd actually believed she could change him. That she could save him. That he could become like her—someone who believed in love. "You couldn't have done any differently."

"Exactly." Laney looked at him with a tearful smile. "I love you," she whispered, reaching up a hand to caress his cheek. "So much."

Kassius shuddered beneath her touch. He felt

choked by competing emotions of fury, regret, agonizing desire and loss—such deep loss!

Looking down at her, he savored the beauty of her
lovely face, the curve of her cheek, her full lips. Her
warm, loving brown eyes, deep enough for a man
to drown in. He took a picture of memory. He knew
this would be the very last time he'd ever look upon
Laney's face.

"Benito is outside. You can wait in the car." He
forced himself to give her an encouraging smile.
"There's air-conditioning."

"Ooh," she said happily, as he'd known she would.
"All right, I'll wait outside." She squeezed his hand.
"Just let him explain. Give him a chance!"

He gave a single nod. It was hard to speak over the
lump in his throat. "Goodbye, Laney."

Patting him on the shoulder, she left. Going to
the far window, Kassius drew back the curtain and
watched her go out into the courtyard. He saw Benito
come up and talk to her.

Dropping the curtain, Kassius turned away. He
couldn't watch what would happen next.

"Cash?"

He turned sharply to his father.

"What happened to you?" the man whispered. He
was staring at Kassius as if looking at a ghost he
was afraid to touch. "When I finally got your letters, I rushed to Istanbul, but no one knew where
you were…"

"Oh, did you finally come looking?" he replied
coldly. "I sent letters for five years."

"My wife hid them from me. She only gave them
to me at our divorce—"

"Yes," Kassius ground out. "Your wife." His lip curled. "Mama always defended you, did you know that? In spite of the way you seduced her with promises of love and marriage, when you knew you were capable of neither."

The older man took a single staggering step back.

"You're—right," he said finally, running his hand over his forehead. "When I fell in love with Emmaline, I was already trapped in a loveless marriage. I hid it from Emmaline, because I knew she never would have looked at me..."

"You're right about that," he said scornfully. "She would have told you to go to hell. But unlike you, my mother had a soul."

"I wanted to marry her," Boris whispered. "I wanted it desperately. But my wife refused to divorce me."

"Liar."

"It's true." The older man's voice trembled. "I begged her. But even though Tania already had taken many lovers of her own, she wouldn't let me go. She knew that with my position I had the opportunity to make a lot of money in the breakup of the Soviet Union. She told me I'd have to pay her millions of rubles to agree to divorce me." He took a shuddering breath. "I tried to make money as fast as I could. But it wasn't fast enough."

Kassius looked contemptuously around the front room, with its faded wallpaper, its missing furniture, its dust. "All the while talking to my mother of the fantastical villa you would someday buy her."

The man swallowed. "I wanted to buy Emmaline her villa. I wanted to live with you, be your father.

Your hero." He gave a weak smile. "Do you remember, when you were young, how we used to pretend to be Roman gladiators, fighting with wooden swords? We sometimes knocked over the furniture. You loved it when I told you stories about the Roman Empire, far past your bedtime, until your mother was furious at both of us…"

A memory floated back to Kassius. It had been his father who'd told him stories of the Romans? Pain went through him. The pain of a boy who'd loved his father, only to be rejected by him, abandoned. It was pain he'd thought he was past feeling, and fury filled him that he was not.

"And you left us," he said hoarsely. "You left my mother to die without help. For five years, you could have come back to help us—could have phoned, sent a letter—"

"She wouldn't let me," his father cried. "When you were eleven, your mother found out I'd been married to another woman since before we'd even met. It didn't matter to her that we'd been estranged for fifteen years, or that my wife had a lover but wouldn't divorce me until I had made a fortune to pay her off. After Emmaline found out, nothing I could say or do would persuade her to let me visit again—or even send her money! She told me to get out and never come back, never try to contact either of you again until I was free to love you both. So I went back to Moscow, determined to finally get the divorce Tania had denied me." His voice broke. "I never imagined it would take me five years to earn enough, because each time my business grew, she only became greedier for more. The only reason she finally agreed to the divorce was that she fell pregnant by her longtime lover. And by then, it was too late." His voice was hollow. "Your mother had already died."

Kassius wouldn't show mercy. "Because of you."

He clawed his hand through his gray hair. "I never knew Emmaline was ill," he whispered. "Not until it was too late."

Kassius reminded himself of the pain he'd felt when he'd seen Boris with his wife in Moscow, living in a mansion, apparently without a care in the world—while his own mother lay dying in poverty in Istanbul. He said tightly, "You still deserve to be punished."

His father looked at him.

"I have been," he said in a low voice. "I spent all those lonely years desperately missing you. When I finally rushed to Istanbul, you both were gone. All I found was your mother's grave. I've spent all these years looking for you. I thought you were dead."

"You destroyed her life."

Tears filled the old man's eyes. Blinking fast, he looked away, staring blindly out the windows. "I thought we'd grow old together. She was the only woman I ever loved. I always meant to go back to her. I just thought we'd have more time—"

His voice choked off.

Kassius stared at him, refusing to feel sympathy.

"Forgive me, Cash," he whispered. His knees collapsed beneath him, and he fell back on the chair. "I never loved anyone again after I lost her—and you. I never wanted another wife, another child. You were both everything I ever wanted, but it was based on a lie, so I lost it all. I tried to keep the business going for the sake of my employees, but to tell you the truth, I never had the heart for business. All I have left—" he looked around the half-empty room "—is this villa. It's all I had left of her. Keeping that promise I'd made to her…"

His voice broke, and he covered his face with his hands. Kassius stared down at the weeping old man.

It was his moment of vengeance, just as he'd dreamed about. He should have felt a sense of triumph.

Instead, all he felt was empty. Boris Kuznetsov was old now. He'd committed the crime of falling in love with a young, idealistic stewardess and pretending he was free to marry her, when he was not. For that, he'd lost everything.

So much had been lost, by everyone.

Kassius had the faint memory he hadn't let himself think of in a long time. His father teaching him in the Istanbul street, when he was a young boy, how to play fight with a sword. How to be a gladiator. How all the other kids who lived on the street had been jealous and fought to be included. How happy he'd been. How proud of his father. His hero.

I was so unhappy. So awfully unhappy. I didn't want to feel that way. So I decided to forgive her. To remember the good times. I chose love…

No. His stomach clenched. He couldn't think about Laney now, on top of everything else.

His phone buzzed in his pocket. He saw Laney's number. Repressing his churning emotions, he lifted it to his ear. "Yes?"

"What's going on?" Laney sounded frightened. "Benito pushed me into the car. He says they're taking me to the airport then sending me back to New Orleans. I don't understand."

Kassius set his jaw. He made his heart very small.

"It's over," he said coldly. "As I told you. I will pay money for your support and nothing more. My lawyer is drawing up the paperwork for our divorce."

In the room, he heard his father's intake of breath at the same time as Laney's.

"Divorce?" she whispered.

"I told you what would happen if you betrayed me. I will never see you again, or the baby."

She gave a long, brittle, anguished gasp. It rattled and echoed across the line. "I don't believe it," she choked out. "You wouldn't be so...so heartless."

"You did this, Laney. *You did this.*"

"Kassius—"

Then her voice cut off with a scream. He heard a squeal of tires, a scream, a crack. And then nothing. A moment of silence, and then a busy signal. Frowning, he stared down at the phone in his hand. Was it a trick? He had to suppress the intense desire to call her back. It had to be a trick. But he couldn't be manipulated so easily.

"You are wrong to treat her so badly," his father said behind him. "All she's done is love you and try to bring us together."

Kassius put his phone in his pocket and faced him with a cold sneer. "*Love?* What do you know about that?"

"I know how it feels to lose it." His father looked at him with tears in his eyes. "I know how it feels to make one bad choice that ruins everything. When Emmaline told me to leave and not come back until I was free, I tried so hard to do it. I told myself I could make up for all the lost years. But the truth is that time is all we possess. Time and love. Choose carefully." His voice broke. "Before you throw it away."

Kassius shook his head coldly.

"My business manager informed me you already canceled the loan you were going to take on this villa. You might have managed to keep this place for now, but I have taken over your bankrupt company and I'll be selling it off for parts. Along with everything else I've taken from you. This villa will be small comfort to you when…"

"It's yours."

Kassius's eyes widened. "What?"

"I give it to you freely," his father said quietly. "The last thing I possess. I built it for your mother, after she died. You are all that we have left. The last memory of our love. Cash, this villa is yours."

For a moment, Kassius couldn't find a voice to answer. Kuznetsov simply giving him the villa was the last thing he'd expected. The last thing he'd wanted.

"Keep it while you can," Kassius bit out, turning away. "My lawyers will be in touch."

Outside the villa, dark clouds had covered the sun. From far away, he heard a low rumble of rolling thunder as a cold wind rose from the sea. He turned his face up to the first drops of rain, relishing the feel of it on his hot skin.

As ordered, his men had taken his wife away in the limo and he was left with the sports car, the key beside it. He was grateful to be the one driving the two-seater, since with the rear-wheel drive and performance tires, it could be a little dodgy on slick, wet roads. He wouldn't want Laney to be taking any risks—

Then he remembered Laney was no longer his problem, since he was never going to see her again. He'd never even see his son born. A pang ripped through his heart. He was leaving her and the baby.

Just like her mother had done to her.

Just like his father had done to him.

Kassius took his phone out of his pocket, testing himself against the savage temptation. He couldn't call her. He *couldn't*. That would be breaking his vow. Revealing his own weakness. He couldn't be weak. He couldn't break his word.

Like a miracle, his phone suddenly rang in his palm. He saw his bodyguard's number and snatched it up. "Yes?"

"Boss, we've had an accident," Benito said hoarsely. "A truck collided into us on the road. Police and ambulance just got here. Lamont's dead… that flask smelled of alcohol. I think it slowed his reflexes…"

Kassius gripped the phone. "Let me talk to Laney."

There was a long silence. "I can't."

"What do you mean?"

"The truck plowed into her side. I wasn't touched. She and Lamont got the worst of it." The man's voice was a whisper. "They're loading her into a helicopter to take her to the Hôpital Princesse Florestine. They're not sure…" His voice broke. "I'm sorry, boss. They're not sure if she and the baby will make it."

Not sure she and the baby will make it…

A haze went over Kassius's eyes. A memory of everything Laney had tried to do for him…trying to love him, to convince him to love her, to even love himself. Trying to make him a better man.

And for that he'd ripped out her heart and sent her and his child away, unknowingly to their deaths...

He staggered against his car. He dimly noticed that his father had followed him out of the villa and now stood beside him in the rain, staring at him with wide eyes.

"Boss?" His bodyguard sounded panic-stricken.

"The main hospital in Monaco?" Kassius whispered.

"Take the north road. Get here as fast as you can."

Turning from his father, Kassius flung himself into the car. Starting the engine, he drove as fast as he could, focusing with hellish intensity on the drive beneath the rain, pushing the sports car to the limit. He crossed the border into Monaco and then roared up to the hospital, parking beneath the portico, leaving his car helter-skelter in front with the door still open.

He ran inside, and his shout carried up and down the hallway. "Where is she? Where is my wife?" he cried. "Where is my son?"

"Monsieur, calm down!"

"Please, monsieur, this is a hospital! Show some respect!" the nurses tried to hush him.

"Where is she?"

"If you don't stop yelling, we'll have you thrown out of this hospital!"

Kassius saw the nearest nurse motion to a hospital security guard, who came forward. He gritted his teeth. Where was Benito when he needed him? Where was Laney?

He took a deep breath, trying to force himself to

remain calm when he felt like screaming and grabbing the nurse by her scrawny neck and forcing her to cough up the information he needed. Wiping his eyes hard, he spoke over the jagged razor blade in his throat. "Please," he said tightly. "My wife was in a car accident on the coast. She is thirty-six weeks pregnant. I was told she was brought here via helicopter…"

"Ah… Her." The nurse looked up at him with pity in her eyes. "I'm sorry, monsieur," she said quietly. "You're too late."

CHAPTER NINE

"Too late?" A man's voice roared suddenly behind Kassius in French. "You tell him this in the hallway?"

Kassius whirled around and saw his father, who must have broken speed records to follow him to the hospital, standing furiously beside him.

The nurse stiffened. "Monsieur?"

Boris had fury in his dark eyes. "Are my daughter-in-law and grandson dead?"

"Lower your voice, this isn't—"

"They were brought here. You either let my son see his wife or get a doctor out here to explain—now!"

Scowling, the nurse retreated to the desk and checked her computer. Kassius waited, breathless with hope that she'd say it had all been a mistake. She'd tell him that Laney was absolutely fine, and the baby doing perfectly well, and Benito had simply made a mistake...

But the woman's eyes only clouded as she saw something on her computer that made her give a brisk nod. "It is just as I thought." Looking at them, she hesitated, biting her lip. "If you please, messieurs, go wait in the waiting room, and I will get a doctor to discuss—"

If Kassius had to wait another second to hear if Laney and his child lived or died, he thought he would collapse. He already felt like he was on a thin margin. To his surprise, he felt his father's hand on his shoulder, giving him strength.

"We're not moving until we know where she is," Boris said forcefully.

The nurse glanced around as if she wished desperately there was someone else they could speak to. Then she sighed. "Your wife is in surgery," she said reluctantly. "That is why I told you it was too late. They are performing a caesarean in an attempt to save the baby…"

An attempt? Just an attempt? "Then she is—"

"That is all I can tell you. Now go—" She pointed firmly toward the large nearby room filled with plain white plastic chairs and televisions blaring the news from Paris. "I will send the doctor to speak with you."

Waiting in the Princess Florestine Hospital waiting room, waiting to hear if his wife and child would live or die, felt like the most agonizing hell of Kassius's life. As he sat down heavily in a flimsy plastic chair, questions pounded through his head.

How badly had Laney and his son been injured? Were they dying? Could his wife already be dead?

They are performing a cāesarean in an attempt to save the baby.

In an attempt.

Leaning forward in his chair, Kassius put his elbows on his knees. He folded forward in his grief and fear, covering his face with his hands.

"She's a fighter, son." He felt his father's hand rest

comfortingly on his shoulder. "She loves you with all her heart. She'll fight to stay with you."

"Why would she?" Pain gripped Kassius's heart. "I told her I never wanted to see her again. I was so angry with her for talking to you. I saw it as a betrayal. I told her I was divorcing her and sending them away." He looked at Boris bleakly. "You heard me."

He heard his father's ragged intake of breath. "You were angry. She knew you didn't mean it."

"She knew I did." Misery swamped through him, shame and anguished grief. He'd threatened to abandon her and the baby and start a new family. *Oh, my God!* He clawed back his dark hair. In this moment, he would have given every penny of his fortune to know they were safe. He would have given his life to be able to hold her in his arms and tell her he loved her!

He…

He loved her.

Kassius's lips parted silently. His heart was beating so fast it felt like it was rattling inside his rib cage. He loved her. And it was only now, when he was so close to losing her, that he realized it. He loved her…

His father's hand tightened on his shoulder. "We all make mistakes we regret. She will forgive, and you can spend the rest of your life making it up to her…"

If she lives. It was the unspoken thought that hung over everything. If she lived. If his baby lived. And Kassius had so casually thrown them away! After she'd disobeyed him, he'd thought he had no choice— as if holding firm to prideful, petulant promises were the true mark of a man!

Loving his wife. Loving his child. Those values were the true mark of a man.

But the realization might have come too late. His relationship with Laney had begun with a car accident. Now, it seemed, a car accident would end it. He'd thought he had eternity to play with. He'd never imagined eternity would end so soon. A memory of his father's voice came back to him.

She was the only woman I ever loved. I always meant to go back to her. I just thought I would have more time...

Kassius looked at his father, whom he'd judged so harshly. He'd spent over half of his life determined to destroy him, but instead of punishing Boris for his crimes, maybe he should have taken a hard look at his own.

"Thank you," Kassius said thickly. "For being here."

"Oh, my boy," his father choked out, "there's nowhere else on earth I could be."

"Monsieur Black?"

The doctor had come in. They both rose to their feet. Kassius felt the floor trembling beneath his shoes. The verdict he was about to get from the doctor would determine if he would live or die. Because his family was his life now.

"Your wife..." The doctor suddenly smiled. "She is out of danger. She's stabilized, but still under anesthesia. She broke multiple bones, including ribs. She couldn't breathe well and lost so much blood. It was touch and go. If the impact had been a little to the right, or it had taken longer for the paramedics to arrive, we might have lost them both."

Grateful tears rose to Kassius's eyes. His heart was in his throat. Wiping his eyes hard, he said hoarsely, "And my son? Is he all right?"

The doctor's smile widened. "Would you like to see him?"

Laney's eyelids fluttered. She woke in a dream.

Golden sunshine was shimmering through tall windows. She was stretched out in a comfortable bed. And there, like a miracle, sleeping in a hard chair beside her, she saw Kassius. His handsome face looked weary, as if he'd had very little rest that night.

"Kassius," she croaked out through dry lips.

His eyes flew open. Leaning forward, he gently took her hand. In spite of the dark circles beneath his eyes and the scruff on his jawline, his handsome face glowed with joyful tenderness she'd never seen there before.

"You're awake," he whispered, gently brushing back a tendril of her hair. "Thank God." He gave a rueful laugh. "It was quite a night."

For a moment, she wondered what he was talking about. She just felt happy to see him. Then realization slowly crept in that she was in a hospital room, wearing a plain hospital gown. Wires were hooked onto her arms. She heard the slow beep of machines nearby. Parts of her body had been immobilized, other parts covered in bandages. Her brain felt strangely fuzzy.

"What happened?" she said slowly.

His dark eyes searched hers. "Don't you remember?"

Laney started to shake her head, but it hurt too much, made the whole room twirl.

"You're still on a lot of painkillers."

Laney licked her lips. "I…"

She suddenly had a dim, chaotic memory of seeing a semitruck skidding across the road, coming straight toward their car. She remembered seeing it bounce off another car and head straight for her side of the limo, where she was carefully buckled in. She remembered the loud squeal of brakes and the angry blare of a horn. She remembered dropping her cell phone and wrapping her arms protectively around her belly, turning away with her eyes squeezed shut as she heard the sickening crunch of metal on metal and felt the impact.

After that, her memory was jumbled. She remembered crying her mother's name, and Kassius's, begging them to help her. She had a strange memory of the *thwup-thwup* noise of a helicopter and paramedics shouting in French and loading her onto a stretcher before the pain was too great. The last thing she remembered was putting her hands on her belly and whimpering, "Please, you have to save my baby…"

With a gasp, Laney put her hands on her belly now. She looked up at Kassius in horror.

"Where's my baby?" she cried.

"Shh…it's all right." Rising from the chair, he went to the bassinet across the room and lifted out a tiny swaddled form. "He's here. Right here."

Returning to the bed, Kassius placed the bundle gently in her arms, on the side of her body that wasn't broken. He kept his hand on the other side of the baby, supporting his weight, protecting them both.

Laney looked down in awe at her sleeping new-born son, swaddled and wearing a little cap to keep his head warm. Tears rose in her eyes as she marveled at his precious little face. "He's all right?"

"Six pounds, four ounces—almost three kilo-grams," Kassius said proudly. His dark eyes were tender as he gently stroked his sleeping son's cheek. "For a preemie, he's a bruiser."

"Preemie." She looked up in a panic. "He came too early!"

"He's fine," he said soothingly. "His lungs are developed enough he doesn't need any extra medi-cal care. The nurses and doctors were amazed. But I wasn't. He has his mother's spirit." He looked at her, and his eyes glistened suspiciously as he glanced at her injured body in the hospital bed. "I know even this won't keep you down for long. We were lucky." Lowering his head, he softly kissed the top of Laney's head, and whispered, "*I* was lucky. To get another chance."

She looked up at him, her heart in her throat. "So you—forgive me? For what I did?"

"What *you* did?" Kassius repeated. For a moment, fear gripped her heart.

Then, keeping one hand on the baby, he fell to his knees next to the hospital bed in front of her aston-ished eyes. His handsome face was anguished.

"You were right about everything, Laney," he said in a low voice. "Everything. And the way I treated you for trying so hard to save my useless soul…" Reaching for her hand, he kissed it, then pressed his forehead against it fervently, like a prayer. "Forgive me. I almost threw you and the baby away for the

sake of my own foolish pride…" He took a shuddering breath, and his voice was ragged, barely above
a whisper. "When I said I would get a new wife, a
new child…"

"You were angry," she said in a small voice. "I
betrayed you."

"You, betray me? Never. You saved me. You were
right about my father. I spent a long time talking to
him last night, in the waiting room…"

"He's here?"

"He didn't want me to suffer alone," Kassius said.
"All these years, he hated himself for lying to my
mother. He was haunted, wondering what happened
to me."

"Do you forgive him?"

"I would have once thought it impossible." He
looked up at her, his dark eyes shining with tears.
"But now…how can I not? He made a ghastly, unfor-
givable mistake. But so did I. Treating you so badly…
Can you ever forgive me? Will you?"

"Oh, my love," she whispered. She tugged weakly
on his hand. "Yes."

He rose to his feet, then leaned forward over the
bed, supporting their sleeping baby with one hand,
cupping her face with the other.

"I love you, Laney. I never knew what those words
meant before, but now I do. I love you."

Her heart skittered as she heard him speak the
words she'd feared he would never say.

Straightening, he stood tall and powerful and
proud beside the bed.

"And I make you a promise. One I will never break.
When I thought I'd lost you, I wanted to die. I knew

then that I'd gladly die for you, and our baby. But now I know you're alive…" He put one hand gently on her shoulder as the other rested on the downy head of his sleeping son. He said softly, "For the rest of my life, I will live for you."

"I love you," she whispered, tears in her eyes, turning her face toward his. And he kissed her.

EPILOGUE

FOUR MONTHS LATER, Christmas had come to the French Riviera with a burst of sunlight and color. And family, Laney thought. Family above all.

They were all there, celebrating the holiday at Boris's redecorated pink villa on Cap Ferrat. Even Laney's grandmother had interrupted her world tour for a weeklong holiday visit, with her current boyfriend in tow. For much of the last year, Yvonne had traveled the world with a backpack, a floppy hat and a total fearlessness that still left Laney in awe.

"My boyfriend is great, isn't he?" her grandmother said archly as the two of them cooked in the huge, bright kitchen.

"Very," Laney agreed. "Everyone likes Ove."

"Handsome. Athletic, too. Energetic. I had to beat back the other ladies on the ship with a stick. But I got him," Yvonne crowed as she stirred the gumbo.

When her grandmother had visited here last month, the Henry women had announced that both Kassius and Boris must give their household staff Christmas off, as Laney and Yvonne would be making Christmas dinner personally.

Kassius had looked overjoyed, then doubtful. "Are

you sure you want to take the trouble, Laney? It's a holiday. You've only just fully recovered. A month ago you were walking with a cane. You should just relax and let someone else work."

"I'm fine now," Laney had protested.

"Let someone else cook for Christmas!" Yvonne said indignantly. "Are you crazy? What kind of fool idea is that?"

So Kassius hadn't tried to put up any more of a fight. He'd just wiped tears of joy from his eyes. He'd been looking forward to Christmas ever since, as eagerly as any child counting down the days until the magical morning.

Thinking about it, Laney gave a low laugh. Her husband appreciated their cooking, that was for sure. Only a few hours now till Christmas dinner, and he still anxiously stuck his head into the kitchen every few minutes, as if that would make the time fly by faster. She'd finally had to banish him from the kitchen when she'd discovered him sneaking in surreptitiously with a spoon.

"What?" he protested as she pointed firmly at the door. "Just trying to help with quality control!"

Still smiling, Laney checked on the cinnamon swirl king cake now in the oven. It was baking nicely. She also had the tiny plastic baby figurine ready to stick into the cake after it cooled, for one of the guests to find over dessert. That person would then be allowed the privilege of choosing where they hosted family Christmas next year. That had been her father's idea.

"It's really the only way to be fair about it," he'd explained, glancing at his girlfriend, who lived in

Atlanta. That was true, since their family now lived all over the world.

Hearing her four-month-old baby coo, Laney lifted him from his baby seat and twirled him around the kitchen until he giggled and squealed, the best sound in the world. He was a brilliant baby, and very good at grabbing his own feet. Clearly, she thought proudly, a baby genius.

"And how is Henry Clark?" her grandmother said fondly.

"He loves Christmas. Don't you, Henry," she cooed, and he giggled back at her.

"Can't believe that husband of yours bought him a puppy for Christmas. A puppy for a baby!"

"I'm suspicious about who the puppy is really for." Laney grinned. "Kassius can't wait until he's delivered tomorrow. Says this is the best Christmas ever!"

"Wait until he experiences Christmas in New Orleans." Yvonne sighed. "It's been lovely to travel, but after all these months, I've seen enough of the world. I'm ready to go home."

The grand new house on St. Charles Avenue had just been finished and was ready for Yvonne and Clark to move in, with a dedicated guest wing for Kassius, Laney and baby Henry to visit. Although there was still some question if Clark ever meant to return.

After months spent at the top medical clinic in Atlanta, cutting-edge medical treatments had partially restored his vision. Laney had wept openly when she'd first tucked her baby into her father's arms and he'd been able to see the color of his grandson's hair, the boy named in part after him. There was some hope he'd eventually gain complete vision in his left eye. He'd never looked better, Laney had thought. He'd looked positively muscular as he rolled his new wheelchair around the Christmas tree that morning, a gift from his daughter and son-in-law, which had made him exclaim over the "kick-ass rims."

Clark had brought his new girlfriend, Jeanie, a nurse from the clinic, for Christmas, too. The plump and pretty divorcée, with two grown children and a grandchild of her own—all of whom were spending the holiday with her ex this year—kissed him affectionately as they finally sat down to Christmas dinner.

Laney looked at her family around the big table spread with Cajun Christmas cheer, mixed with some French breads and wine and even some Russian borscht and vodka, thanks to Boris, and felt tears in her eyes. After so many years of despair, they were all happy. They were together. A Christmas miracle.

Even Kassius's father looked fifteen years younger. His son had insisted he continue to keep this as his home, and all the sold-off furniture had been replaced and, except for Mimi, all his laid-off employees re-hired. His oil company had been folded into Kassius's worldwide portfolio as a loosely held subsidiary, and with the influx of new investment and technological innovations, there was hope for the company's future.

But Boris was happy for his son to run it now. All he wanted, all he'd ever wanted, it seemed, was his son, and to be part of his family.

"Aha!" Yvonne said, holding something up triumphantly. It was the tiny baby figurine. "Next year, Christmas in New Orleans!"

Everyone looked at her suspiciously.

She widened her eyes, the picture of innocence. "What?"

"Sabotage!" Boris cried, waving a jar of hot-pepper sauce. "That's what!"

"It was pure luck!" she protested.

No one believed her, but they just laughed. Everyone was happy, and it was impossible to hide it.

Life had once felt so dark for all of them, Laney thought as they shared Christmas dinner around the table. Each of them had lived through a different kind of pain. But for each of them, love had melted it away.

Kassius had done it, Laney thought suddenly. He'd changed their lives. He'd been the miracle.

But when Laney told him as much, when they'd all risen from the dinner table to take a family walk through the villa's beautiful, well-kept gardens, Kassius snorted and shook his head.

"If there was a miracle, it all came from you, Laney," he said as a cool breeze whirled around them from the sparkling blue sea. He glanced back at his father, who was smiling tenderly at his baby grandson harnessed to his chest in a baby carrier, walking with Yvonne and Ove and Clark and Jeanie. Turning back, Kassius tucked a tendril of her long dark hair behind her ear and said seriously, "It all started with you. Your courage, and wisdom, and grace. From the moment we met…"

She tilted her head teasingly. "You mean when you hit me with your car?"

He grinned, then sobered. "I'm just sorry I made you go through far worse pain than that." He looked down at her, his dark eyes deep with emotion. "But you didn't give up on me. You loved me, even when

I didn't deserve it. You always knew I could be the man you deserve. The man who loves you. The man who always will."

She swallowed over the lump in her throat. She felt so happy, it brought tears to her eyes. "Kassius…"

"Wait." Abruptly, he pulled her away from the rest of the family, into a small copse of oak trees behind the box hedge. Looking up at the oak tree, he said innocently, "Oh, look…mistletoe."

Astonished, Laney looked up at the evergreen leaves and white berries growing on the oak tree. Then she narrowed her eyes.

"You lured me to this spot on purpose," she said accusingly.

He lifted a dark eyebrow. "Would I do that?"

"Totally."

Kassius grinned. "You know me well." He ran his hand slowly down her back. "So you might as well know, I intend to lure you into bed later. Maybe more than once."

Eyes shining, Laney reached up to caress her husband's rough cheek.

"You don't need to lure me," she whispered. "Just kiss me. And never let me go."

So lowering his head, that's exactly what he did.

* * * * *

If you enjoyed this story, look out for these other
great reads from Jennie Lucas
A RING FOR VINCENZO'S HEIR
UNCOVERING HER NINE-MONTH SECRET
NINE MONTHS TO REDEEM HIM
THE SHEIKH'S LAST SEDUCTION
Available now!

Coming soon in the WEDLOCKED! *series*
A DIAMOND FOR DEL RIO'S HOUSEKEEPER
by Susan Stephens
Available November 2016

#3477 ONE NIGHT WITH GAEL
Rival Brothers
by Maya Blake

Aspiring actress Goldie Beckett smashes billionaire Gael's dating rules when she storms into his board meeting! After discovering her pregnancy, Gael won't let his son be illegitimate. Gael must get Goldie to agree to the role of a lifetime—*his wife!*

#3478 SNOWBOUND WITH HIS INNOCENT TEMPTATION
by Cathy Williams

Becky Shaw didn't expect to spend Christmas warming herself in the arms of Italian billionaire Theo Rushing. As a snowstorm rages outside, indoors the temperature's rising. It's meant to be a holiday fling—until Theo reveals he needs a fake fiancée!

#3479 A DIAMOND FOR DEL RIO'S HOUSEKEEPER
Wedlocked!
by Susan Stephens

Don Xavier Del Rio is determined to claim the inheritance given to his aunt's housekeeper, Rosie Clifton. So when Rosie surprises him with a marriage proposal, Xavier sees a way to get everything he wants...including Rosie in his bed!

#3480 UNWRAPPING HIS CONVENIENT FIANCÉE
by Melanie Milburne

Violet Drummond can't face another Christmas party alone, but Cameron McKinnon seems like the perfect plus one. Until he reveals his plan to make Violet his convenient fiancée! Cameron needs to escape unwelcome attention, but soon fake feelings shift to real attraction...

YOU CAN FIND MORE INFORMATION ON UPCOMING HARLEQUIN® TITLES, FREE EXCERPTS AND MORE AT WWW.HARLEQUIN.COM.

HPCNM1016RB

"I'm sorry. I'm out of here."

"Dante…"

"No. Listen to me, Willow." There was a pause while
he seemed to be composing himself, and when he started
speaking, his words sounded very controlled. "For what
it's worth, I think you're lovely. Very lovely. A beautiful
butterfly of a woman. But I'm not going to have sex with
you."

She swallowed. "Because you don't want me?"

His voice grew rough. "You know damned well I want
you."

She lifted her eyes to his. "Then why?"

He seemed to hesitate, and Willow got the distinct
feeling that he was going to say something dismissive,
or tell her that he didn't owe her any kind of explanation.

HPEXP1016

But to her surprise, he didn't. His expression took on that almost gentle look again and she found herself wanting to hurl something at him…preferably herself. To tell him not to wrap her up in cotton wool the way everyone else did. To treat her like she was made of flesh and blood instead of something fragile and breakable. To make her feel like that passionate woman he'd brought to life in his arms.

"Because I'm the kind of man who brings women pain, and you've probably had enough of that in your life. Don't make yourself the willing recipient of any more." He met the question in her eyes. "I'm incapable of giving women what they want, and I'm not talking about sex. I don't do emotion, or love, or commitment, because I don't really know how those things work. When people tell me that I'm cold and unfeeling, I don't get offended— because I know it's true. There's nothing deep about me, Willow—and there never will be."

Don't miss
DI SIONE'S VIRGIN MISTRESS,
available November 2016 wherever
Harlequin Presents® books and ebooks are sold.

www.Harlequin.com

HARLEQUIN
Presents®

***Christmas might be a time for giving,
but in Lynne Graham's festive new duet
Christmas with a Tycoon, two Mediterranean
billionaires are thinking only of what they can take!***

Italian tycoon Vito Zaffari is waiting out the festive season
while a family scandal fades from the press. So he's come to his
friend's snow-covered English country cottage, determined to
shut out the world.

Until a beautiful bombshell dressed as Santa literally crashes into his
Christmas! Innocent Holly Cleaver sneaks under Vito's defenses—he
wants her like no other woman before and decides he *must* have her.

When Vito finds her gone the next day he's sure she'll be easy to
forget…until he discovers that their one night of passion has a
shocking Christmas consequence!

Don't miss

THE GREEK'S
CHRISTMAS BRIDE

December 2016!

Stay Connected:
www.Harlequin.com

www.IHeartPresents.com

f /HarlequinBooks

🐦 @HarlequinBooks

📌 /HarlequinBooks

HP13488

Whatever You're Into... Passionate Reads

Looking for more passionate reads from Harlequin®?
Fear not! Harlequin® Presents, Harlequin® Desire and
Harlequin® Blaze offer you irresistible romance stories
featuring powerful heroes.

⧫HARLEQUIN *Presents*

Do you want alpha males, decadent glamour and jet-set
lifestyles? Step into the sensational, sophisticated world of
Harlequin® Presents, where sinfully tempting heroes ignite a
fierce and wickedly irresistible passion!

⧫HARLEQUIN *Desire*

Harlequin® Desire novels are powerful, passionate and
provocative contemporary romances set against a backdrop of
wealth, privilege and sweeping family saga. Alpha heroes with
a soft side meet strong-willed but vulnerable heroines amid a
dramatic world of divided loyalties, high-stakes conflict and
intense emotion.

⧫HARLEQUIN *Blaze*

Harlequin® Blaze stories sizzle with strong heroines and
irresistible heroes playing the game of modern love and lust.
They're fun, sexy and always steamy.

Be sure to check out our full selection of books
within each series every month!